Greg Gannaway

And The Mountains Cried

A Novel by

Greg Gannaway

In memory of my mom and my dad,
and
my wife, Emy

CONTENTS

Part I

Matt Callahan

CHAPTER   1

There are many mysteries in the world, from the stars in their multitudes to the creation of life; from the way an artist brings color and wisdom out of himself, to the breathless rush of lovers, whose hearts have shed the weight of worry, and believe everything, accept everything, and for whom no distance on earth is so far away as tomorrow.

So what can be said about a man and a woman who feel that they, of all the other men and women in the world, belong together? Can it be no more than a chance encounter, of simply living on the earth at the same time? Is it only the curve of the neck, a thoughtful glance, the sound of the voice, the way the eyes are set? Or is it something hidden, mysterious, something beyond an encounter, beyond fate? Could there be others, in other places, other times, whom they might have loved and who might have loved

them? Can there be but one person among all others---
among all those who have ever lived, from man's
beginning until time's end---to whom they are drawn,
and for whom they must search and must love until
death? Perhaps reading this story will help you decide.

It was late September 1992; the weather had
turned. The wind-washed bowl of the sky closed on
the earth, a metallic gray, bringing the first full relief
from the Texas summer. For three days it had rained
non-stop, cool and heavy. Now the rain had stopped.

Sitting at his drawing table, Matt Callahan wished it
would begin again---he listened, but there was nothing,
only the sound of the forest outside, and in his cabin
the sound of silence. Pressing himself against the back
of his chair, he turned to the drawings stacked before
him, lifting one sheet, then the next, then another. It
was a house design, drawn on broad sheets of white
tracing paper, black letters at the bottom of each sheet
forming: *RESIDENCE FOR JAN HARRIS*. He was
about to call her when something caught his eye. Part
of the design thought to be so simple and functional
seemed no longer so. Something wasn't right, too
complex; he would call her later.

He didn't get the chance. The phone rang just as
he was reaching for a roll of sketch paper. Picking up

the phone, he glanced back once at the drawings before answering.

"Matt."

From the voice he knew immediately who it was.

"Hello, Jan," he said.

"I haven't heard from you in a while. I thought you were going to call me."

"Sorry, Jan, I ran into a little problem. I'm working on it now."

"When can we meet?"

Matt thought for a moment. "How about eleven o'clock tomorrow morning?"

"At your place, okay? I want to see where you've been hiding out."

It was strange, Jan always wanting to see where he lived. When she asked him why he had given up his home in the city to live alone in the country, he toyed a moment with the question, giving her a steady, polite look. "I don't find it lonely, Jan," he said. "For me it's just a better way of living."

He went on to explain how he found it easier to assemble his thoughts when gazing out into an expanse of wooded grassland than when faced by a tassel of neighbors. Jan said she'd like to see it sometime. When he told her all it had in it was a king size bed, a few chairs, a drawing table, a forty-inch TV, and was twenty miles out of Austin, she said, "Are you going to show me the place or not?"

For Matt marriage was something he hadn't thought about since his divorce, but he suspected Jan would like to set up housekeeping and give it another try---with him.

"Matt, are you there?"

"Yes, Jan, that'll be fine. See you here in the morning."

The decision ran against his better judgment. Shaking his head, he closed the phone, turned back to the drawings and began to study each section meticulously. It occurred to him that the problem might be in the framing and, turning to a sheet of structural drawings, he quickly saw it.

"Ah ha," he said aloud and rose from his chair. Rolling out a length of sketch paper, he began to draw, his hand moving freely, flexible as wire, slashing quick, bold strokes across the paper. He paused for a moment, studying the sketch, walked away, came back, he was wide-open. Where next, he wondered, but he knew where next---everything had become silently clear.

Again he began to draw, then, suddenly, he stopped. From the corner of his eye there was motion, something was moving along the creek beyond his window. His glance hesitated halfway between the movement and the sketch he was drawing. He turned back to the sketch. Still it did not satisfy him. He tossed the concept, let it wander off to die and returned his glance to the motion outside.

And The Mountains Cried

All was silent; stillness hung in the air, a waiting stillness swept clean by the splendid animal standing motionless in the tall grass, head high, watching, listening. Leaning back in his chair, Matt felt himself slowly draw down into the quietness, tension draining away like water from a trough. In that moment, while it lasted, time's passage was sweet. The moment held, flickering, as if in a light wind.

The deer stood like a monument, then suddenly jerked his head upward and, in one smooth, arching leap, raised his one hundred and fifty pounds over a wire mesh fence and disappeared, as if a shadow, across the creek and into the brush. There was the faint sound of splashing water, then no sound at all.

Matt looked into the silence, caught the breath of the moment and slid it into his memory. It was but another reason for living by Bear Creek, on fifty acres in the hill country of Texas. It had been his home and office for twenty five years.

Matt too had heard the heavy shoes on the deck of his cabin. Swinging around in his chair, he turned to the knock at the door, his pencil dangling precariously between the tips of his fingers. Through the glass door, against the low light of evening, he could form no specific image of the face, only a thick neck and a slightly rounded stomach, shoulders stooped, like the silhouette of a tapering jar. When a heavy voice with the strong hint of the Mexican border said, "Hi, Champ," Matt recognized Juan Sanchez.

Greg Gannaway

Juan had always called him Champ, a vestige of Juan's days as a boxer. He spoke the name effortlessly, in a tone drawn from all their years of working together; a tone of admiration. Matt had grown to like the name, guessing the alternative would have been to call him chump, which he didn't think much of.

"Was that Samson?" he asked. Juan had seen the deer.

"Yeah, that was him."

"He's gettin big, Champ…how old you think he is?"

There was a flicker of light and shadow as Matt swung his arm from beneath his desk lamp, tilted his chair back and paused for a moment's remembrance.

Samson had become more than a wild animal. Star attraction was a better description, a spirited contributor to the affairs of the place. He was tall, sleek, the smooth pelage of his back and sides was predominately brown and gray, flowing into soft white along his chest and belly. Standing in the swaying grass, he was a blend of nature, the forest, underbrush slipping green from his shoulders, his great antlers gleaming in the sun, their conformation perfect.

But, for all his size and strength, he was seldom conspicuous, instinctively staying hidden in the brush, his shape dissolving into the colors of his surroundings.

And yet there were times when he did step out, clear of the trees, into the open sunlight; and in those moments there was no escaping his presence. Standing on legs clean as steel, he was a vision of freedom and power and beauty---he was a vision demanding to be seen.

"I suspect he's close to five."

Juan stood silently for a moment, his face still, except for a slight narrowing of his eyes, as if against a strong light. "Hard to believe ain't it, Champ...it's a wonder he's even alive."

Matt nodded his head. It was true, Samson's mere survival in this land of hunters was, in itself, a triumph. But Matt had raised him to go as he pleased, to enjoy the changes of the seasons, the days, the nights, taste the wild grasses and all the other recurring pleasures that came with being free. It was the life he was meant to live, wanted to live, and that's the way it would always be.

He remembered first seeing Samson in the small field behind the cabin, no more than two weeks old, weak and scarcely able to walk. Matt had watched him for several minutes, then returned to fetch food. When Matt climbed over a dry-stacked rock fence and made his way slowly to the little fawn, who watched him all the way, head wobbling back and forth, until his trembling legs collapsed beneath him and he fell to the forest floor, Matt was able to come right up to him and gently stroke his neck. Then, with the proficiency gained from helping his grandfather nurse orphaned calves, Matt guided the little fawn until, with tail twitching, he had sucked the bottle dry. He hoped that would give him strength and send him along to his mother. But the next day the little fawn reappeared at the front of the cabin. He looked at Matt with soft brown eyes, as if to let him know that his mother would never return.

Matt had always believed that life must include concern for things beyond one's self, of living harmoniously with nature. The roaming honey bees, rabbits, ringtails, the great hawk soaring in a wind's full distance, flowers and trees, rivers flowing to the sea, he fashioned the idea of living alongside them rather than above them. And so it was with the little fawn.

Sensing he was not in harm's way, the little fawn straightened his ears at the touch of Matt's hand, not in fear, but rather from a position of trust, and through the red and yellow sunsets of the years that followed, he would ask for nothing more.

"Any trouble on the job?" Matt asked.

"No, Champ, but I would like to talk with you."

Juan glanced at the drawings laying face up on Matt's table, pausing, as if to apologize for his unannounced visit.

"Finished Miss Harris's house yet?" he asked.

Matt nodded his head. "Yeah, she's coming by in the morning. What's up?"

Several days ago Juan had come to Matt and said he needed to speak with him. Then he left without further explanation. Matt had detected a slight edge of uncertainty in his voice and began to wonder if something was wrong. Juan had not approached him again until now.

Juan removed his hat and walked across the open room, placing his big, red knuckled hands along the edge of Matt's drawing table, his face weather-browned, lined by age and wind, evidence of his sixty-four years in the sun.

He had come down a winding foot path connecting his cabin with Matt's. He did this sometimes to visit with Matt. They would discuss the progress of a job or a particular construction problem and afterward talk of the normal routines of life, often telling each other outrageous stories and laughing like children.

But today would be different. Juan leaned closer against the table, the light falling on his stubble cheek, gray threads glistening. Held snuggly beneath his arm as if a private treasure, was a worn oil cloth folder and, in one of those rare moments when a person of meager means feels the world to be a better place because of something he possesses, he opened it.

Across Matt's desk, all executed from the first word to the last official stroke of ink, he spread a survey drawing and title to a five acre tract of land in the mountains of Monterrey, Mexico.

"My father left it to me," he said.

Matt let his fingers carefully trace over the survey. It was a simple document; black lines, strong and hard, pressed into fading white paper. Yet touching it, running his fingers along its lines, Matt began to feel as if a living piece of earth had been laid across the table.

His immediate glance found a small black rectangle in the center of the drawing, marking Juan's boyhood home. Juan had lived there with his family until he was sixteen, then headed north across the Rio Grande.

Texas was as far north as he got. Juan's first job had been washing dishes in a large restaurant. But he soon discovered more satisfying opportunities and began working in the construction industry, his name preceding him from one job to the next as a hard worker.

When Matt first met Juan, the man had spoken in broken phrases, yet the tone of his voice cut across the handicap, polite, friendly and strangely persuasive. Matt had remembered hearing the name linked to such things as extra effort, loyalty and listened quietly. After a short interview, Matt had given Juan a job. Within a year he became Matt's construction superintendent and had moved into one of the guest cabins on Matt's acreage.

Juan arrived at work early every morning, inspecting each structure with meticulous scrutiny. The men loved him, but they also knew what he expected of them---no excuses. If a man worked hard, he needed nothing more to gain recognition, it was given to him, not as a gesture of kindness, but because it was earned. Juan asked about their families, where they attended church, their home life, brought lunches for those who had none. He responded to the essence of their being, their working capacity. It bred a feeling of gratitude and loyalty and, in the end, an immense feeling of self-respect within every man on the job.

Matt sat at his drawing table, watching Juan with a gentle, deeply felt respect.

"I've got something to ask you, Champ,"

Matt inclined his head, catching an edge of uncertainty in the tone of Juan's voice. Folding his hands together, he looked up and ask: "What is it?"

For a minute Juan said nothing, trying to place the moment into some orderly sequence of time. In his memory the past years held only the sweetness of time, being the happiest of his life. It had been the small pleasures of living along Bear Creek that, in its simplicity, he would never forget. Often, when driving down the pasture road in the breaking light of morning, he would see Matt standing on the deck of his cabin, waving, "Morning, Juan," and he would call back through the open window of his pickup, "Morning, Champ," with a broad grin on a face filled with gratitude. On cold mornings there was just a tip of the hat, Matt standing inside the door, Juan with his windows up, each making sure the other was okay for whatever the day would bring.

"It's time for me to go back to Mexico, Champ," he said. He spoke in a low, flat voice, almost as if trying to sooth his own feelings.

Matt stood and walked to the big rock fireplace at the far end of the cabin. He didn't want Juan to leave, but had always known that someday it was going to happen.

Juan's eyes followed him, an open glance, curious, waiting. A cast iron pot hung low over a small open flame. Matt lifted the lid from the pot and, clutching a heavy metal spoon, stirred its contents. The smell reached him in an instant, as the aroma of pinto beans rose through the room.

"Are you sure this is what you want to do?" he asked.

"I'm sure, Champ." Matt did not turn, but kept his gaze directed at the small, crackling flame, white flakes occasionally fluttering into the air. He knew Juan deserved easy chairs and a restful future, but he also knew this was probably not his friend's plan.

Juan waited as Matt walked back to the table and sat down. He looked straight at Juan, letting him see the full attentiveness of his face.

"Anything I can do to change your mind?" Matt asked.

Juan hesitated and Matt saw a faint movement of his head, the kind of movement with which one contemplates an answer that comes with tormenting pain. "No, Champ," he said, his voice trailing off, as if abandoning sound.

Matt's eyelids dropped and, for a moment, there was only silence. Then Juan took a deep breath and began to speak. He spoke of his family and friends, easing each word forward as if held by some fragile thread that might break away at any moment. So much was there---poverty, yearning, grief, sorrow, love---told in terms that pulled Matt into a world Juan had never before mentioned. Inside his eyes Matt saw the pain, heard the tone of his voice fall across the still air of the room and knew that such recollections came from a place deep within his memory, his soul, and heart.

"You ever been deer hunting, Champ?"

"Years ago, back when I was a kid."

The last time Matt had gone deer hunting he'd been sickened from seeing the poor animal gasping and frothing on the forest floor, its shoulder blown away by the terrible blast from his rifle.

"Animals got a right to live same as we do...only thing I kill now are mosquitoes and scorpions...and that's only when I find them in the house."

Juan took a long breath. "I used to go with my brother," he said. "We only hunted to help feed the family."

The telephone rang. Matt motioned to Juan and reached across his desk. "Hello." There was a pause and Matt chuckled, "No, Jan, eleven...that's right, yes...see you in the morning."

He turned back to Juan. "Sorry about that...do you ever hear from your brother?"

Juan sat staring out the window. There was a soft wind outside, sweeping along the banks of the creek.

He saw the thin branches of an elm tree swaying, like arms waving in a cry for help. The tree stood against the glow of a late evening sky.

He could not name his sudden emotion. Some of it was relief, hushed, like the act of kneeling. When he turned back to Matt, he tried to smile, but the smile never appeared.

"No, Champ…that's why I left Mexico. There was an accident."

"What happened?"

To this day Juan could not say for sure just what did happen. In fact, much of it he could not remember. That he and his brother had left the house before daylight; that he told his brother if they killed anything, it would be nice to share the meat with their neighbors, then the frightening horror of seeing his brother tangled in a web of tree limbs, blood gushing from his chest, his thin arm reaching out helplessly, struggling for life, for another day, another moment; of holding his brother's hand and not knowing what to do, the feeling of being unable to breathe and shaking violently. And later the piercing cries of his mother and father. The sorrow was suffocating, deep, unbearable.

The funeral was held in a small, white church nestled along a wooded mountain road in Chipinque Park, not far from Juan's parents' home. The church had filled early, a mass of friends and family, some pressed against the walls, their faces solemnly raised to the pulpit, where the priest commenced with the services. One of the faces, pale and stunned, was Juan's. He sat in the front, trying to keep his eyes on the pulpit, because he knew people would be looking at him. He did not look back. Three days earlier, in the half light of early dawn, he had fired his rifle at what he thought was a deer and killed his brother.

Matt had never doubted the nature of Juan's character, but now he began to realize that no matter how hard a struggle Juan had lived through in his youth, he had never abandoned his will to act. Even in moments of tragedy, he had never let suffering and poverty win its victory, never allowed it to destroy his inner core, his desire for joy, his desire to live.

Juan stood by the drawing table, his eyes moved first, then he leaned his head in and looked down at the survey for a long moment, to Matt's face and back again; an unconscious gesture of asking, of reaching for something that had yet to be said.

Matt pulled his chair closer against the table, leaning forward, his forearms resting comfortably on the desk, his two hands clasped together before him. He looked at Juan quietly, a hard, clean glance of understanding.

"I'll help if I can," he said.

Juan straightened himself, focusing on that one desire within him; no, even more than that---the seeds that planted the desire; that dream, rooted in his mind, growing, as if feeding on its own existence; a vision that was always with him.

"Have you seen it in me?" Juan asked, his voice rising slightly.

Matt had faint memories of what he had seen in the past: of Juan standing along the edge of the deck looking out across the pasture into the trees. He could remember something happening to Juan's eyes---a change from a glance to a distant gaze, as if his eyes were no longer seeing the trees, but something beyond, a wisp of thought, like a dream he was trying to grasp before it faded from view.

"Perhaps…"

Juan stood without moving, the flesh on his broad face was rigid, his mouth slightly drawn, but now his eyes were calm and held the certainty of the words that were to follow.

"Do you know what I've always been afraid of, Champ?"

"What?"

"Poverty."

Matt looked at him, puzzled. "But that's over for you."

"I suppose, but it's still out there. Champ, we were dirt poor and nobody cared. That's what scared me…that nobody cared…not enough to lift a finger."

Beyond the intense look in his eyes, Matt saw something within his friend he had not seen before, something hard and hurt.

And The Mountains Cried

"It's my family and friends, Champ, they're poor, yeah, but they're not evil...know what I mean? They're hopeful and good---it's poverty that gives them no chance in life. I want to give them that chance, a place where they can communicate and deal and live...give them houses with decent comfort, a place to enjoy their family, you know...where they can feel safe." He paused and shook his head. "It don't figure, just cause a person is poor don't mean he doesn't have dignity." He glanced back at Matt, then turned away, his eyes reflecting times he did not want to remember.

"No one should be without hope...should they, Champ?"

There was a distinctive break in his voice, the muscles in his face moving, for an instant, in an expression of pain and Matt knew that his friend had known the reality of every word he spoke.

"That's my dream, Champ," he said. "That's what I carry with me, I..."

Again he hesitated. Matt saw that he still stood as when he had entered, his forearm resting against the table at the same angle, the wide curve of his hand spread open, relaxed, but his face seemed to have contracted into the stress of times past.

"Take it easy, Ol' buddy..."

Juan looked at him, his face drawn, he tried to smile. "...I need your help, Champ." His voice held the tone of a man teetering along a narrow ledge, slow, anxious, groping for just the right spot. "Can you help me, Champ?" he asked. "You know I can build 'em, but designing 'em, drawing the plans, placing 'em on the site…" He sighed and shook his head. "It…it's something I just couldn't do."

Matt sat back in his chair feeling the emotion of the moment. The final break in Juan's voice revealed that the request had not been an easy thing for him, and that without Matt's help there would be little chance of the houses ever being built.

He stood up, put his hand on Juan's shoulder and smiled with a confidence that had always given Juan comfort. "Your idea is good…I think we can work out something here."

Juan stood relieved; no words, no work accomplished had ever made him feel more exuberant and alive. Matt saw two eyes looking at him with immense gratitude, and visible from the corners of Juan's mouth, like two bright points of light, was the beginning of the happiest smile Matt had ever seen on Juan's face.

"Thanks, Champ," he said.

Matt nodded his head. "First thing I'll have to do is take a look at the site."

Juan stood drawn up for an instant. Matt caught a glimpse of his face: it held a sudden look of surprise.

Juan knew how to build a house; he did not know the process of designing one, nor did he realize that his request would call for Matt to make a trip to Monterrey.

And The Mountains Cried

But Matt took control, leaving him no time to wonder. "Think of it as a retirement gift," he said, "for all your hard work. Besides, I love Mexico. The trip will do me good."

Working together over the past twenty years had given them a special sense of each other. Their understanding of construction, their enjoyment, their work ethics were of the same nature, the same source, creating a mutual trust and respect that had never wavered. Matt thought of Juan as family. Since Matt's mother died, there had been no one else. Driven by caution, Matt had conscientiously set up a savings account for Juan and invested the money in various stocks. Over the years the investments had grown into what now seemed to Juan a virtual empire.

Matt got two cold beers from the refrigerator and indicated for Juan to move a couple of chairs over to the fireplace. A light wind moved across the pasture, rippled the grass, died as it slipped past the deck of the cabin. Matt gave the beans another stir and threw a fresh log on the coals. It smashed into the flames and sent sparks flying against the sooted rock. Then he settled back and listened while Juan spoke of the houses, of the thoughts behind the idea, of thoughts that shaped his life, spoke deeply, like a man thrown into space, flying, grabbing the air in huge, clean chunks.

Darkness would soon be slipping down to fill the valley, when Juan stepped off the deck of the Matt's cabin.

"Champ," he said, waving goodbye, "if you get lost, drive toward the mountains. You can see them from anywhere in Monterrey." Then he turned and disappeared down the wooded path, his shadowed footprints trailing in the brown dust.

Matt walked back inside the cabin and made a turn through the room. He saw his own figure approach him in a panel of glass doors. The loose fit of his clothing did not reveal the structure of his body. It had the raw, tensile strength of a sprinter; lean, angular, as if formed from an artist's casting. His face had the precision of fine sculpture---high cheek bones, a full mouth faultlessly traced, with blonde hair about finely hollowed temples. His eyes were perceptive, intelligent, the deep, dark blue of light falling through water, clear and steady. He gave little thought to what people said---that he looked younger than his 47 years.

He moved forward, letting his eyes focus beyond the glass, into the dim light along Bear Creek. The creek took its life from hidden springs twisting down through the wooded hill country. It was wide and cool, vibrant with the sounds of wild life that followed a network of game trails to drink in the late evening. The water moved in a gentle ripple over a limestone bottom, its surface reflecting the earth in multi-shaded colors. He wondered why such a tranquil scene would make him think of it now, that sense of apprehension without reason. No, he thought, not apprehension, more than that: a mysterious, inner threat, hidden in the shadows, lurking, unexplainable.

It seemed nothing had recalled it, but he thought of it, of his childhood in Austin, his mother, of what he had seen and did not want to remember. He felt anger at himself, he had to stop this, there was no reason that he should remember it on this late evening.

He had never understood the problem, he knew only of its consequences. It was his dark side, a hurtful side, from which he had never been able to detach himself, as if his personality, his talents and strengths were of one person, his irrational fears of another.

He had told no one of the ordeals, not even his closest friends, knowing they could never understand. Indeed, they would not even recognize it to be him, as if seeing a photo from which only the outline of a shadow was visible.

He stared absently into the trees, Had he always felt it? Yes, at least as far back as he could remember. It seemed to have stemmed from the constant cycle of fear and panic he had lived through as a child. But now he was no longer a child and still, under certain conditions, it came upon him, a causeless, mystical dread, without foundation or reason, and that he had suffered terrible pain and guilt from all of the occasions and opportunities lost from this inexplicable fright.

In those awful moments, the back of his neck would stiffen and he couldn't think logically. Was it simply a defect in his makeup---like flat feet or headaches? It was a question he could ask, but not answer.

Wild ducks began circling over the elm trees along the creek, peering through the branches for a place to land. Matt conscientiously straighten his shoulders, then raised his eyes and watched as they let down through the twilight, rippling the water as they landed.

And The Mountains Cried

C H A P T E R   2

That Matt Callahan was going to be an architect
was never in doubt to anyone who ever knew him.
There were things he knew and no one knew just how
he came to know them. He understood the philosophy
of design as a painter understands the harmony of
color.

By age ten, he was working part time as a laborer
in the building industry, assisting framers, plumbers,
electricians, doing anything he could to learn the
different aspects of construction. After school, he even
began to sketch out basic floor plans and elevations of
small houses.

His mother used to like telling how, at eleven years
old, she'd found him at his desk early one morning, a
soda bottle turned over on its side in a dark puddle,

Matt's arm in the puddle, his head resting on his arm, fast asleep. And stacked neatly to one side, she said, were the plans of his first house, neatly drawn and complete.

He was born in Taylor, Texas, an only son. His mother, Margaret Callahan, worked in a department store, outgoing and vivacious. His father had been a farmer, hardworking and steady, telling anyone who'd listen that he could plow a furrow, build a barn and handle a team of mules as well as any man.

But when Margaret was five months pregnant, her husband's tractor rolled back on top of him in a mud-filled corn field. Matt was never to know his father.

"Not ever knowing my father left a vacant place within me that I have never been quite able to fill," he would later say.

As Matt grew older, he began to think more and more of how his father had died so unexpectedly. The idea that life could be so fleeting, so brief, seemed always to be with him, driving him to be more conscientious, to work hard and do well to honor the father he never knew.

Seven years after her husband's death, Margaret married a jaunty real estate agent called Ned Munson. With six year old Matt in tow, the couple moved to Ned's home town, Austin, Texas.

Compared to Taylor, Austin was paradise, a beautiful city on the Colorado River, drawing people from across the country to its lakes and warm weather.

And The Mountains Cried

Margaret took to Austin immediately, exuberant in her new life. She was a gifted artist, who liked to cook and, without quite realizing it, dress herself to be looked at. She had won beauty pageants before Matt was born and he still thought she was pretty. It was like getting the highest grade in class, or catching the biggest fish to have a mother who looked better than the others. Many were noticeably overweight and had lost pride in their appearance, wearing baseball caps and stretched-out T-shirts over faded jeans, with little or no makeup. Margaret Callahan did not look and she did not dress like the others; her hair was always styled and she never left the house without makeup and jewelry, seemingly born to look no other way, as if this were her place, her moment---she was energetic, she was fun, and she was beautiful.

Outwardly Matt seemed to be living the everyday American childhood, sunny and bright. Learning came easily for him. He taught himself to draw at the age of six. He drew everything he saw, stunning his teachers with displays of work beyond his years.

But inside his frame house on Bridle Path, he was leading a far more frenzied life. The face of his mother, that once shimmered with so much love and beauty, was now a picture of fear and sadness, as her marriage deteriorated into arguments and screaming matches that spread through the air like poison. She had gambled on a new start the way she lived---with everything she had, her first husband loving her and

Matt with a feeling and concern that Ned Munson could never imagine. Now, as he descended into alcoholism, he grew more and more violent, striking out at Margaret in fits of rage. The incidents were always with Matt, deep down, like a long-held breath he could never release.

"…Childhood is supposed to be a happy time," Matt recalled one evening while visiting with Juan. "But is it truly…I don't even like to think about mine. There was so much anger and fear…" As he spoke, Matt leaned forward, his eyes looking straight at Juan, but his mind had drifted back into the past and he thought about the long path that had brought him here. Who was he then? And who was he now? On the surface, the answers were simple. His name was Matt, and he designed buildings for a living. And though the answers were true, he knew a closer look would reveal the guardrails and barriers that, in many ways, had restricted his life. For all the things he'd done, there were many more he had opted out of, frozen in his tracks by the threat of what felt like true insanity. He would feel especially anxious at social gatherings, poised to run from the room at any moment.

The origin of such behavior was unclear, but it seemed, at least in part, to have stemmed from the turmoil of his childhood.

He turned away, shaking his head. "Sometimes I think I made it up, that it never happened. It…it was like I wasn't going see the next moment, much less live through it."

Juan could not classify the expression on Matt's face; it was one he did not recognize, as if he was trying to blast such memories from his mind.

As a child of an alcoholic, there had been a part of Matt's life so shaken, so filled with pain, he shared it with no one. The horror began soon after the family moved to Austin. Oh, he'd heard his mother and step-father arguing a few times, but up until that point, life within the family had been fairly routine. Then one night, in its darkest hour, he was awakened by the screams of his mother. Before he could even process what was happening, the impact of a blow from his step-father sent his mother crashing into a wall. He could only squeeze his eyes shut and shiver from fright.

After a time, he began to have nightmares, terrible, recurring nightmares, always the same one, in which he would witness his stepfather beating his mother. He became frequently anxious in his classes at school, as if the classes were happening to someone else who happened to be him---a someone in a state of torture.

His teachers and classmates had no clue as to the turbulence in which he lived; a despair rumbling through him, his small soul suffocating in darkness. He became adept at hiding the ugliness of his home life, the anger, the shame, living an external life that people could observe, but inwardly suffering in silence the fear and anxiety of a boy who had seen his mother being abused again and again.

It had occurred to him over the years that the best way to deal with his future would be to simply pretend the fear and ugliness of the past did not exist. He would go to school, be cheerful, optimistic, be upbeat, and simply block it from his memory as if it had never happened.

With fierce enthusiasm, Matt threw himself into his new life. Austin High had never seen anything like him. During the next two years, he became somewhat of a local celebrity, excelling in track and field. People would speak about, 'that beautiful boy,' remembering the grace and speed of his movements. His mother, who had almost vanished into obscure poverty before divorcing Ned, even stopped worrying so much about him. But for all of his accomplishments, Matt still found himself trying to redeem and rescue himself, instinctively arranging his life within a particular comfort zone, tending to avoid activities or circumstances that would stimulate his unexplainable fears.

He had been in school on the morning his mother was found bleeding, her nose broken, beaten almost unconscious. She was lying on the bedroom floor when found. No one knew how she had managed to drag herself to the phone and call for help, but she did; the medical emergency crew discovering a trail of blood on the carpet upon their arrival.

And The Mountains Cried

When his teacher told Matt that his mother was in the hospital, she saw his eyes become puzzled and helpless, his breath fading into a choked moan. He slumped down in his chair, not moving, his hands clasping the sides of the wooden seat under him.

After a moment, he raised his head, "Thank you for telling me," he said, and walked out of the classroom. The appreciation was sincere, but the teacher knew there was something different in the tone of his voice; something cold, and very frightening.

Matt walked the four blocks to the hospital. The light in his mother's room had been dimmed. His eyes moved first, an intense glance, like a long thin beam held fast at one end, its point holding firm to the bandages covering the left side of his mother's face. After a moment, he gathered himself and walked to the edge of her bed, trying not to show the shock of what he saw. It was too late: there was a faint smile on his mother's swollen lips, a resigned admission of what had happened, and he understood that it was much worse than the other times.

After several minutes, he heard the doctor quietly say she had suffered no permanent damage, but they should let her rest.

When Matt stepped out into the hall, a young nurse, slightly built, stopped him on his way to the elevator and said suddenly: "I had a mother…once. She was beaten too…like yours, but she died." Something had made her say that, and she looked at

Matt, not quite certain she had done the right thing. But Matt smiled and turned to her, placing her hand in both of his. He was not sure if he grasped the exact nature of what had been said, but he could see the pain in her eyes and felt certain that she knew of his. It made him stand silently for a long moment, facing her. Then he said: "Thank you," and walked away.

Matt did not go back to school that afternoon, he walked; he had to walk, to feel movement, to help control his anger and the furious contempt he felt for himself for allowing his mother to fall victim to more violence. He walked for an hour, through a park to a jogging trail along the river, crossed over a foot-bridge and through a narrow stretch of woods where, at the end of a long path, was a hidden rocky bluff.

He knew this was where he wanted to be, because for eight years, ever since he was nine years old, it was the only place he had found to escape the truth of his home life, to be alone, to forget, to feel alive, and to find comfort.

From the bluff he could see the river below and across the river the city stood up hard and dark against the horizon, its distant sounds falling and fading in the air. It was a day in November, the sky was gray. Far below, the water caught the cold tone of the sky in a shade of green. Matt stood at the edge of the bluff, the ghostly images of days past wrapping round him in solitude and silence. There was no strain, no effort in the stance of his body, but his face was unyielding. He was now seventeen years old, his body hard, lean, his face cut by a few sharp lines; the lines were not a reflection of his age, they were the lines of rage.

He stood for a long while without moving, looking blankly across the river at the buildings merging with the sky. But this was not the sight in his mind and, in a sudden fury, he beat his fist together in futile disbelief. How could he have let this happen again?---knowing that it was another in a long line of violent days that stretched back into his childhood and, that if he did not act, it would happen again.

He knew now what he must do. There was no need to think of it any longer, everything was clear, the choice was simple, like a problem with only one answer, and he wondered why he had not fixed it long ago.

He felt the wind in his back; the wind made the day seem colder. He shivered and stepped back from edge of the cliff, wrapped his muffler around his neck and swung back down the narrow trail through the trees, across the foot bridge to a long, wide street stretching off beyond eyesight; the cold mist of fall drifting along beside him.

'No more,' he cried soundlessly into the fog around him, 'no more.' The thought made him shudder; he clenched his fists and walked faster, the sound of each step driving the words into the cold, wet sidewalk.

Greg Gannaway

He stopped, a traffic light hung in the air above him, a spot of red in the misty wetness. He stood and watched a small sports car go by, its wheels skimming over the slick, gray asphalt of the street. The light turned green and he went on, seeing nothing around him. No more---it was the only conscious thought in his brain---no more…no more…no more…

The mist was turning to light rain as he approached the grassy edge of a familiar sight. It was Lions Golf Course, a course he had played several times and knew well. He cut straight across the 14th fairway, down a winding road, to Bridle Path where, at the end of a gravel drive, stood the white frame house where he had lived ever since moving to Austin.

Ned Munson was alone, sitting hunched over the breakfast table in a corner of the kitchen, reeling, tiny beads of sweat swelling on his forehead. He did not hear the sound of Matt's steps when he entered the house. He heard them only when Matt came into the kitchen.

As he lifted his head, so intense was the light crashing into his red, sunken eyes that he involuntarily closed them and began to blink. When he opened them again and his eyes refocused, there was Matt, nothing more than a child only a short time ago, now looming in a crisscross of light before him, a tall, lean muscled young man, his face drawn, grim, his lips closed, set tight.

And The Mountains Cried

Munson coughed once, then again, then a third time, before trying to speak, his thick, pink tongue moving in and out between his teeth.

"Ah...Matt, listen, I'm sorry, things just got a little out of hand. It...it was a mistake, okay...how bout we just forget the whole mess."

Matt shuddered and wondered whether Ned Munson's brain had gone soft, then told him how things were going to be, his voice cutting through the heavy air with but one brief, concise demand---That Munson leave.

"And if you don't leave voluntarily," Matt concluded, "I'll break your head open."

He waited. Munson sat still, his pale, bloodshot eyes blank, his mouth agape, a line of phlegm dribbling weakly down his chin.

"But I don't want to leave, it won't happen again...I'll quit drinking, I promise." He said it meekly, pleading, in a whiney little voice.

"You're leaving."

"But I don't want to...I won't." He leaned forward and whispered slyly: "You might not know it, but I'm going to be famous one of these days." He giggled softly, "and rich too."

"I don't think you're getting the message, Ned. You're outa here."

"Well, I'm not so sure of that...and besides..."

It was only a second's pause, but it seemed to Matt, that Munson had given his final answer and it was an answer that did not please him. He was not in the mood to hear anymore and started toward him.

Munson grabbed the almost empty whiskey bottle from the table. At the moment when he rose to his feet and drew his arm back ready to strike, Matt leaped straight at him, as if hurled by a giant spring, knocking the bottle out of his hand, the glass bursting into pieces against the wall.

He had only his two fists, but it seemed his body had been transformed into something no longer human. Blows smashed into Munson's body, his face, spattering blood against the walls and floor. In an instant he was on his back, and when he looked up, Matt Callahan was unrecognizable; he saw only a whirl of motion suspended above him. It was the last thing he saw. Something happened to his jaw and his head struck hard against the tile floor.

When he regained his senses, groaning on the floor, Matt was standing over him, arms hanging at his side, fist clenched, still on the edge and ready to go at him again.

"Have I made myself clear?"

Munson struggled to his feet, he stood awkwardly, bent over, clasping the edge of the table. He felt himself shaking, a shade of fear in his face; he wanted to vomit.

Watching Matt come at him again, he tried to move away without turning his face, not wanting to look into his threatening eyes, but Matt seized his right arm by the wrist and twisted it behind his back until the arm nearly turned in its socket. Munson began to struggle and scream from the pain, and only when Matt released him from the terrible hold and threw him out of the house, did his howling pleas die away.

Three months later, Matt's mother was granted her divorce. It was not contested and Ned Munson was not present at the brief hearing. He was never seen or heard from again.

That year seemed like the crossing of a frontier which ended Matt's childhood. At age eighteen, after graduating from high school, he went to work for a large architectural firm, Top Notch Design. He worked part time while attending the school of Architecture at the University of Texas.

For five years this was his life. He lived at home with his mother, having little time for anything other than going to school and working. She watched his progression into manhood, supporting him at every step, but felt the life he was leading to be a lonely one. He had a few friends, but none who were close, and he had girls, but spoke little to them of love, feeling that any relationship between them was understood. But by his own account, most of the time he wasn't working or studying, he was analyzing the real estate market, driving through different parts of the city looking for property he could develop.

She noticed that he'd grown quieter, even shy at times, and, although pleasant to be around and open to conversation, spoke only when he had something worth saying. There was nothing sad about his quietness. It seemed more a kind of relaxed confidence, as if it had been with him always.

Once he graduated from college, his advancement was swift among the employees of Top Notch Design. As an architect he felt free to be himself. He took pride in his accomplishments, but each advancement was more than an accomplishment to him, it was a symbol of his pride, of his struggle, of his ability to achieve, of his rise. It was his time and at every step he took a position of responsibility. He told people what to do and they did it. He took charge long before he was given the authority to do so. He did not have time to worry about titles; when there was a job to do, he got it done. It allowed his superiors, who owned the firm, more time to visit with potential clients and bring in new jobs.

His mother was astonished by his success, and very proud of him. But her years of marriage to Ned Munson had taken their toil and she began to spend much of her time in bed. Matt noticed that her mind would wander from time to time and saw sadness in her eyes when she looked at him.

Then, one evening in February, she reached to answer the telephone and collapsed on the living room floor. Matt was twenty-five years old when she died. 'No one could have asked for a better son,' was the last thing she said to him; her soft glance binding the elements of gratitude and love into one.

As time went by, people began to hear about Matt Callahan. It seemed he had entered his kind of world and for a time the thought of not working for Top Notch Design seemed something he did not hold as conceivable. But in the months that followed, there was a change, and he began experiencing dim thoughts of opening his own office. He was surprised to find that each time the idea flashed across his mind, he would feel a sharp little twinge of excitement. It got him thinking, but he wanted to let the idea ride out a couple of months before making a final decision.

Meanwhile, after work, he began going to the Waterfront Bar and Grill, a favorite watering hole for the single crowd. The reason he kept going back was because he became attracted to a beautiful girl from a little town in the panhandle, she wrote songs and sang there on Friday evenings. He went once a week, for four weeks in a row, always on a Friday, before he even spoke to her.

She had dark eyes shaped like almonds, and long black hair that glistened in the low light. Matt watched the way she moved when she sang, her hips and shoulders swaying in rhythmic circles, smooth and effortless.

On the fifth week, he spoke to her during one of her breaks and she looked at him with eyes that kept on coming. He waited afterward, until she finished her last song. As he was paying his tab, she came up and kissed him lightly on the cheek, then took his arm without saying a word.

Her name was Aponi, it meant Butterfly. She was a far removed descendant of the great Comanche war chief, Buffalo Hump. Later that night, in his bedroom, Matt thought he'd died and gone to heaven, conscious of nothing but the woman before him, of her two hands unfastening the buttons of her dress, simply, slowly, one after the other, of her turning to look at him as she stepped out of her clothes, standing naked, waiting, wanting him to see all of her. Her face was soft, giving it a distinctive form of innocence, clean and young. He walked to her, and when he held her, he could feel the shape of her body pressing into his, and her arms willingly encircling him, feeling the taunt muscles of his back under her fingers. She felt his arms around her; his mouth on hers, and she arched herself into him, adding her hunger to his own swelling need.

She brought him home for Christmas. Her parents lived on a twenty-acre farm just outside the little town of Pachuca, raising corn, chickens, a small heard of angora goats they sheared for mohair, and a Jersey milk cow. They were a proud, handsome couple; both full blooded Comanche of the Penateka band. Matt got along well with everyone, even the livestock and said that he'd been thinking of moving to the country himself. Aponi's mother could tell what her daughter was thinking just from the look on her face: that she'd had her fill of country living and for sure didn't want to spend the rest of her days on a farm.

Several weeks later, when Matt told her that he had bought fifty acres, with three run down cabins along a winding creek twenty miles out of Austin, she was furious.

"You mean you're going to move out in the sticks and quit being an architect," she said angrily.

Matt said he wasn't going to give up his practice, but, yes, he was moving to the country. They were standing in his living room and she whirled to face him. There was a kind of bright, violent look on her face. It had an odd, primitive quality and he saw her eyes narrow as she waved her arms in the air.

"What about this house…" she said, "and your work, don't you even care about that anymore?"

He thought for a moment. "Of course I do," he said. "That's why I'm quitting Top Notch."

Matt walked to his desk, his hand pointing to one of his drawings. "When I'm working there, I can't wait to get back to this. That's when I'm happy…when I care."

She held his glance deliberately, quietly, for a long moment, wondering if he had included her in his grand scheme.

"What about us…" she asked, "did you ever think of that?"

He fell silent and looked out across the room, then down at his fingers spread before him.

"How come you and I never got married?"

When he looked up at her, there was no denying the tenderness he saw in her eyes, the sadness.

"You never asked me," she said softly.

And so he did, and they were married five days later, both secretly wondering if it was a mistake. But her parents had no such feelings, and when Aponi told them the news, they were elated.

For the better part of the first year of their marriage, they lived on Bridle Path, while Matt remodeled the cabins and built their new home in a cluster of trees, overlooking Bear Creek. He took pictures of each phase of construction, painted a watercolor of the finished house and turned it all into a book. On the day they moved in, he greeted her with the gift.

Once they were settled in, he went back full time to his work and Aponi continued to sing at night. In the evenings he would drive her to gigs and wait in the audience until late at night, listening to her, then get up each morning before daylight.

It was on a Tuesday morning, a month after they had moved into their new house, that Aponi received her first request to perform out of town, a two night singing engagement at a club in Houston with a name band.

When Matt arrived home that evening, she took him by the hand and walked him out onto the deck.

And The Mountains Cried

He did not ask why. He sat silently beside her, not noticing that she still held his hand.

"What is it, Aponi?" he asked.

"I have an offer to sing in Houston," she said hesitantly "...for two nights."

Matt sat up slowly and turned to face her. He made an effort at a suitable expression, but his face looked bewildered.

"When did this happen?"

"This morning, Oh, Matt, it's what I've dreamed of, I didn't think it would ever happen, but it has."

He withdrew his hand, simply, without resentment and looked out beyond the creek. There was nothing special to see beyond the creek, only the quiet light of late afternoon on the roof of a small cabin and, above it, the gray sky of a cloudy day.

The effort by which he turned to her was like the slow, resistant turn of a wheel, as if he were contemplating a question of which the answer he would not like. "I want you to be happy, Aponi," he said quietly. "I want it very much. This is a decision only you can make."

After that there were other requests and her absences---sometimes four or five days at a time--- were hard on the marriage. She wanted to see him take pleasure in their time together and accept her being away from home. She saw no acceptance. She saw only the hint of pain, and a situation where happiness did not exist.

He suggested they get away for a while, take a vacation. So they drove to Port Aransas and after a couple of days on the beach, they began to laugh again. They went deep sea fishing and to fine restaurants and shopped and waded in the surf at sunset. But when they got home nothing had changed.

It was impossible for Matt to travel with her. He had been busy from the first day he opened his office, working with clients in Austin and throughout the hill country. She knew that, but kept hoping dimly that it could all be managed.

Spring came and it was the wettest anyone in the hill country could remember. In a deluge of rain, Bear Creek surged down the valley and washed one of the cabins from its piers.

When the rains quit, Aponi told him she was moving to New York to record and study voice.

"I'm sorry," she said, and Matt just nodded and kissed her and took her in his arms.

"Me too," he said.

Five days later, when he returned home from a meeting with one of his clients, she was gone. The note read:

My Dear Matt,

I wish I could have been the one for you. I was—almost, but almost isn't enough for a lifetime. I wish you only good things, take care, Aponi

....Matt, there was something else and it may sound utterly absurd, but let me say it—sometimes,

especially when we were close, I would have this strange feeling that you saw me as someone else, someone in your future that you had yet to meet. I don't know why, but I thought you should know....

He signed the divorce papers two months later. She had asked for nothing but her freedom.

CHAPTER 3

Jan Harris stood in a spread of sky and trees at the front door of Matt Callahan's cabin, the sun on her bare arms, her legs, tracing the edges of her red hair, light and fuzzy, like a halo. Her white dress flared out from the band of her waist, its thin texture emphasizing her abundant thighs. She was of average height, with a narrow face and eyes set close together; a single diamond glittered from a small gold necklace, conspicuously expensive.

Her first meeting with Matt had taken place three months earlier over lunch at the Four Seasons Hotel. After being seated, she sat quietly for a moment, looking at him rather curiously, as if trying to grasp some earlier thought of which she could no longer remember. Then she spoke right up.

"Matt," she said, "I would like for you to be my architect. I need no further time to decide. I'll tell you what I want in the house and the rest is up to you."

And The Mountains Cried

Matt leaned forward in his chair, surprised by the sudden offer. "Is that it…wouldn't you like some references?"

"No, I've already seen what you can do. Look, I have no idea what kind of contract is needed between us, so have one drawn up and let my lawyer look it over, will you?"

"Yes…and thank you, Jan," he said, shaking his head, "…ah…do you always decide things so quickly?"

"Why, yes, I guess I do…all the interesting things anyway, the big things." She said it gaily, without concern.

When Matt began to speak about the design of her house, he spoke with conviction, his voice clear, but after a few minutes, he began to think he was talking to no one. He noticed Jan's face had become blank, expressionless, as if no longer a face, only a pale, empty shell of impenetrable flesh, for which his words held no meaning. In a pause between sentences, she interrupted him.

"Don't try to explain," she said finally. "I would never understand anyway. I have no interest in design theories. Whatever you decide is fine with me."

Then she began to speak of other things, sporadically, her head moving in impatient little twitches. "Actually, I have no idea why I even bought the lot, but I have it now, I wanted it at the time and I bought it, as simple as that, or my fool real estate agent bought it for me…you'll have to meet him, he's a real hoot."

Matt felt mystified by the statement and wondered why she had chosen him. She had never told him the reason. It was a long series of things, a friend who knew someone who remembered someone whose house Matt had designed. After driving by the house only once, Jan Harris needed no further convincing.

A week after their luncheon at the Four Seasons, they met on five different occasions at her lot overlooking the city of Austin and Lady Bird Lake. Matt would bring his drawing pad and make quick sketches of different areas of the site. She did not ask what he was drawing, and stood at a distance while he worked, looking out through the sharp angles of sunlight filtering through the trees, at the skyline of the city, and silently glancing at him with mindful attention; at the angular planes of his figure, his effortless motion, an instance that seemed to give his body the same arranged purity as the drawings he made.

Matt noticed that she had a peculiar way of sliding into questions, almost too casual, yet faintly insistent, as if the questions were a way of encouraging a relationship that might reach beyond the boundaries of business. She asked not about the house, but of other things and would listen to his every word with breathless attention, as if he were the most interesting man in the world. She had told him, with a gentle glance, that she had a condo overlooking the beach at Padre Island and stressed early on that she was divorced. She had her points, all right, he thought, but had missed being beautiful. He guessed her to be around thirty-five, and probably divorced more than once.

But she was pleasant enough and objected to nothing regarding the design of her house, nodding in silent acceptance to anything Matt suggested. She would look at him softly and smile, hoping that some reflection of her hidden thoughts remained within her eyes. He answered all of her questions, his voice polite, steady, but as he spoke she would see an odd flicker in his eyes, as if to tell her there was a wide separation between her thoughts and his.

During their last meeting, he had told her that in the next few days he would need to revisit the site, but that there was no reason for her to come again; that he had all the information he needed and that his next step would be to complete a final set of drawings.

She glanced up at him, studying his face. After a moment she asked, "Shall I tell you what a wonderful job you're doing, Matt?"

She saw his mouth broaden slightly, opening into a smile that never fully materialized. Then he nodded, his blonde hair falling forward, so that she was unable to see fully his face.

"We're fine here, Jan," he said. "I'll call you when the plans are ready."

Greg Gannaway

In the days that followed Matt cut himself off from the world, vowing to see no other clients until the drawings of Jan Harris's house were completed. There was lightness in his movements, composed and intense at once, the swiftness of his hand moving in mechanical perfection along the edge of his parallel bar, pressing crisp black lines onto the white sheets of paper. He would work late into the night, deriving a pure, clean joy from the drawings before him, a sense of freedom, as if lifted from some undefined pressure. He was content, he was himself.

There were times he worked all night. Juan found him still at his desk on one of those mornings. He had stopped by on his way to work to pick up an extra set of prints.

"Champ," he said, "you're unbelievable."

"How's that?"

"It's hard to understand why you're not exhausted. Stress is a killer, you know."

The suggestion of a smile on Matt's face held surprise. "It's when I'm working," he said calmly, "that I feel no stress.

It seemed every wild critter on the place had come out to meet this stranger with the red hair. Squirrels chirped, disrupted from their morning forage, birds flew about feverishly, pumping their smooth wings and turning their feathery heads in sharp little jerks.

And The Mountains Cried

Jan Harris stepped from her car onto the deck of Matt's cabin with a rather noticeable swinging motion, as if to signal her arrival. As she knocked on the double-glass front door, she heard a slight crackling of grass at her back. Turning to see the cause, her eyes went wide, the movement in her face running to her lips, their moist redness pulled open and she wanted to scream, but there came no sound, the certainty of her demise reduced to a breathless echo of silence.

When she entered the property, there had been another creature aware of her arrival, aware the minute she drove through the gate. Samson had followed this strange car through the pasture, stalking its every move. Whenever a tree or bush obstructed his view, his head would jerk impatiently to find it again. He had to look, just as he always had to look at something abnormal. He instinctively knew who his friends were and who were his enemies, knowing always when the stakes were life or death. He had never set eyes on this car, he did not know it; he did not know the woman with the red hair.

Hidden in the shadows, he had watched as she stepped onto the deck. Then, with the slow, assured step of royalty, he walked quietly up behind her. He now stood, swathed in sunlight, only eight feet from her, head high, his massive horns filling the sky.

His eyes were dark and bold and unafraid; for this was his home and she was the stranger, a kind of reversed equality where her place in the scheme of things suddenly seemed less secure than his.

She tried to move but, as if struck by some single, dull blow, her legs went slack. Matt opened the door quickly, waving his arms in an effort to shoo Samson away. It did no good. Samson stepped closer and lowered his head, looking neither to one side or the other and, breathing through widened nostrils, filled his lungs with the unfamiliar smell of the woman, releasing the air in short, quick snorts. For a moment Matt actually thought he was going to charge. But--- perhaps moved by the alien scent---there suddenly came the spring of earth under his hoofs and, smooth as silence, he swung his powerful body into a long, curving leap and was gone.

Jan tried to straighten herself, still jolted by the panic that had run through her body.

"God, where did he come from? He's huge…he scared me to death."

"I'm sorry, Jan, I should have let you know. That's just Samson. He's a pet…I raised him from a baby. Are you okay?"

She glanced at him hesitantly, as if to leave herself open to his concern. "I'm okay now…I think," she said, trying to regain her composure. "He just caught me by surprise." Then she fixed him with big green eyes and her smile appeared fully.

Matt stepped back, feeling a sense of relief that she was okay, held the door and they walked inside. He led her through the cabin to a wide corner of the room, where shafts of sunlight hit the natural grain of a cedar wall. At first glance it seemed austere, unadorned. She gave notice to the sparse furnishings, a ceiling of exposed beams, but mostly she was aware of the clean sweep of space that opened before her, its simplicity, the light spreading over the room, accenting its beauty, bending in radiant delight over every object. The place had the efficiency of an early Texas cabin reduced to essential needs, but with the simple splendor of modern achievement.

They sat together at a long polished table by a line of windows framing a spread of land along Bear Creek. Matt had always found solace in the view. He laid the plans and a large watercolor perspective across the table, letting the morning light hit them straight on; the pure white paper reflecting the geometrical patterns of the design, sharp black lines lifted upward, clear and precise.

She had been only vaguely aware of how her house was to look when finished. During her time with Matt, most of her interest had been directed at him; the design of her house being of little concern. Now she looked at the drawings, at him, curious, and a little astonished. It seemed as if, in that split moment of time, Matt and his work were inseparable.

Matt turned to her. She saw his eyes fixed on her politely, but there remained a peculiar sensation in her mind, an afterthought, as if in the deeper beliefs of

Matt's being he had no awareness of her. She could not explain it, only that she always felt it in his presence, as if a line had been drawn beyond which she was not allowed. Matt asked nothing of her and granted her little more. But when he looked at her with understanding or when he smiled, she felt the pure joy of a woman whose consent he had only to ask.

Jan Harris's house was designed to stand on a bluff above Lady Bird Lake, a flowing mass of stone and glass, rising and falling in a series of horizontal rectangles. The rectangles followed the broken ledges of the rock, stopping, then continuing, each a separate room leading to the final expression of the next, as if the slow progression of the ground had been pulled upward, stressed, and blended into the final shape of the house.

After a moment she asked, "Why do I like the design of my house so much, Matt?"

He looked at her, a cautious half-smile on his face. She imagined in its reflection something beyond the smile.

"Look at it," he said, "notice the structure...how every detail fits one idea."

He leaned forward, drawing her attention to the Watercolor perspective.

"This is the dominant mass...every part of the house is there to support it, to give it balance. The shape is determined by the spaces within, and those spaces are determined by your needs. It's a simple matter of form following function."

He explained the logic of the design, the reason for the house's placement on the site, how it would fit into the surroundings.

After talking for less than an hour, it was clear to Matt that Jan would accept anything that was presented to her, that she had formed no opinion of how the house should be. As he finished speaking, he asked whether she found the design of her house suitable and noticed that she seemed not to have been listening to anything he had said, but to some distant whisper of her own thoughts.

"Is anything the matter, Jan?" he asked.

She looked at him with a kind of expectancy not appropriate for the moment. "I'm listening, Matt," she said, putting her hand on his arm. "I love the house."

She had said she was listening, but it seemed not to the words he spoke, the expression on her face reflecting only a wonder of his talents and something a little more erotic.

He looked at her politely and smiled---a suppressed smile that never fully appeared. Glancing at the door of his bedroom, he thought of how encounters of this type had ended in the past. He knew it would be easy, the woman had been coming on strong ever since they first met. He could only shake his head, feeling the moment's approach to something that had been with

him for a long while: that having sex with every
woman he met belonged to the fantasies of his youth.

"I'm not the answer, Jan," he said.

There was a sound of consideration for her in the
tone of his voice, but his words made her realize that
the connection between them was only a thin wire that
had been broken with the completion of the drawing,
and that with every passing minute he was moving
away into a place where she was not allowed.

She sat before him, helplessly silent and removed
her hand from his arm, taking a moment's pause to
gather her emotions, and to tell herself that it was time
to say goodbye. Then, in a quiet, even voice she said,
with the wink of her eye, "You'll never know what you
missed."

Matt carried six sets of prints out to her car and
said he would send her the final bill. As he said goodbye, she gave him a look, in equal measure, of the
indignity she was feeling from his rejection and that
the design of her house should be proclaimed winner
of some unnamed contest.

He watched her drive away, thinking of the city to
which she was returning, of the naked, sharp angled
masses of stone and glass, of cars moving along the
asphalt streets. He had become impressed with the
new energy of Austin; still he was glad he didn't live
there. For his money, living in the country was the
winning ticket, and held within the peacefulness of his
surroundings was the stub to prove it.

And The Mountains Cried

Over the years Matt had met other women like Jan. They had come to him in similar situations, putting on brash little acts, pretending to be awed by his talents, spilling large amounts of flattery for obvious reasons. It seemed they were all searching for something, trying to fill their lives with whatever they didn't have. For a few, real estate seemed to be the answer. In the spark of a minute, they would buy themselves a big, expensive piece of ground, more often than not paying above its market value. Then after the passing of a couple of weeks and the excitement of the purchase had faded, so would their enthusiasm. They would suddenly realize they had spent a ridiculous amount of money on a lot for which they had little use.

It was never clear to Matt just how they even became involved in such transactions, but, in some fluky manner, it seemed to come about like a law of attraction, each drawn to the other, as if by some spiritual necessity---and in the end they would find themselves hard up against the gnawing question: 'What next?'

Once the possibility of the property reselling receded into the distance, they would come to Matt's office, struggling to find a reason for their actions, looking for what, at times, had turned out to be an odd combination of guidance and consolation. Matt was not one to mix the two, but in the past, in his restless, foolish youth, he had listened, not necessarily to what they were saying, for some of it was nothing more than silly confessions or just careless chatter, he could not decide which, but to the soft, sweet sounds of their feminine gentleness. He could recall a dozen faces, now dimmed, almost forgotten, that he wasn't for sure just how much guidance had been involved, knowing only there'd been no lack of consolation, before and after the guidance.

It wasn't that nowadays he walked away from every opportunity---he didn't, there was a woman or two he saw occasionally, but the trace of desire he felt for Jan Harris was no more than a twinge of physical uneasiness. He had seen the consequences of becoming involved in such situations and the inevitable trouble that followed. Once things went sideways, it was like trying to untangle a roll of barbwire. It had taken him a while to realize this; to learn that within the mind of every person existed a distinct world, different from all others, with their own weaknesses and frailties, and that rarely did people bring the same expectations to these encounters. He had wondered what made them such as they were. He wondered again, thinking of Jan Harris.

It was a bright early fall day, deep blue and sun-yellow. Matt looked into the sky and hoped tomorrow would be the same, then walked back inside his cabin and began to pack---he was leaving for Mexico the next morning.

Part 2

ABBY CASAL

Greg Gannaway

And The Mountains Cried

C H A P T E R   4

$\mathbf{A}$bby Casal awakened in her Monterrey townhome to the muffled roar of traffic rising from the streets below. The sounds were a reminder of where she was and that within a few hours she would be leaving for her mountain home in Chipinque. It was a house given to her by her father before she had married John. She was going without any real purpose, only to meet with friends that, on this rare occasion, she had invited for coffee. Her mind was relaxed because she knew there would be the best of care for John during her absence.

She stood at the window, arms at her side, looking over the rooftops and streets held within the wide frame of glass. A light rain had fallen earlier, but it had passed; the sun a disc of gleaming copper. She could see the mountains from her townhome, they rose upward from the depths of the earth, range after range, like great shadows across the land, a wondrous mystery of creation, bursting into the sky.

The sight made her tingle. It was a strange sensation that seemed to come at unexpected times, old dreams running along the edges of her mind. She would experience dim flashes of them when walking down a city sidewalk or when having dinner with friends or when she woke in the night. She could give no identity to the feeling, only that it drew at her heart and gave a kind of distance to the look in her eyes…and sometimes filled them with tears. Garza Garcia, with its stimulus and beauty, its limitless flow of people, was where she lived. The mountains were home to her heart.

John had never understood her attraction to the mountains and when she would mention to him that she was thinking of going, he would turn and look at her quizzically. She would see the hollows of his cheeks draw in and his mouth would open and, with one sharp intake of his breath, he would utter: "Again." But after a few minutes had passed he would smile and, with eyes soft and mellow and understanding, wish her a safe trip.

Now he was suffering from the ravages of Alzheimer's and she had watched as, over the past couple of years, his mind had begun to slowly disconnect from the person he had once been, from his dreams, his memories, and from her. The progression was slow and painful to watch, but there was nothing she could do, nothing anyone could do.

"I'll only be gone a few days," she quietly told the nurses. Then she leaned down to John and explained that she was going to the mountains. He tried to stand, but couldn't manage it. He dropped back into his chair and looked up at her. The expression on his face was one that had become more and more apparent over the past months---bewilderment, as though something had been said to him that he did not understand, but with which he felt he should agree.

Abby's house in the mountains was an easy drive from her townhome, about an hour, and she arrived a little after one. The house stood alone on a hillside spreading across several long, horizontal acres rising gradually in terraced gardens and interlocking floors; only the woods and open sky stretching beyond. There were no neighbors.

She parked the car in the garage, tapped the horn lightly and watched as Josie came smiling and waving with joy to meet her. She and her husband, Pedro, who attended the grounds, lived in the servants quarters some distance from the main house. Josie was Abby's devoted maid, the keystone of all domestic activity at her mountain home. But she was more than that. Maybe it was the loss of her mother at such an early age, or maybe her growing loneliness, but over time,

Josie had become like a second mother to her. It was with Josie that she shared her dreams of life as she had once imagined, and it was in this house that she was able to confess her growing belief that, somewhere along the way, her choices in life had taken her down the wrong path.

Josie appeared quickly, her half raveled braids showering about her shoulders in graying-black curls. Pedro, followed close behind, eager to assist, but always shy at seeing Abby on her arrival. Still he was quick to help, wanting to spare his wife any heavy work.

Pedro reached down, lifted the suitcases from the car and followed Abby and Josie through the kitchen and up the wide stairway to the bedroom. Josie motioned to Pedro and he placed the suitcases on the edge of the bed. She helped Abby unpack, hanging her dresses in the large closet, smoothing and folding blouses and setting shoes in a neatly displayed row. She left only the fragile lace folds of Abby's nightgown laid out across the bed. Abby felt good at having everything folded and put away and thanked Josie.

"Would you like me to get you some iced tea, Mrs. Abby?"

"Oh, Josie, yes…please."

It had been a busy day, not that she was tired, but it would be nice to snatch a minute or two. That would give her time to call and check on John.

And The Mountains Cried

She sat on the couch, dialed the number to her townhome and spoke to one of John's nurses. John was asleep. Abby thanked her and sank back into the couch, her eyelashes closing over her dark eyes, arms cradled together in her lap, as if trying to protect herself from hidden feelings.

Over the years, before his illness, John's banking career had grown steadily and, in some respects, their lives had settled into a predictable pattern. But John's work began to take up more and more of his time. Work increasingly became his first priority. Abby realized this was why he was successful and a part of her respected him for it, but it wasn't enough. She had dreamed of something more, something different, candlelight dinners, quiet conversations, romance, or something as simple as being together.

They had been married for almost sixteen years; it was 1976 when they met, the economy in dire need of help, everyone simply trying to survive. Abby was teaching psychology at the University of Monterrey, wondering about her life. She had been dating a math professor, who taught school by day and, during the night, greeted her with an array of cocktail parties, each bearing a close resemblance to the other, where both the people and conversation had passed from her memory before the night was concluded. It was not the life she sought and when John, with his comfortable ways and graying temples, introduced himself at a New Year's Eve celebration, Abby knew her affair with the math professor was at its end.

John was a bank president, stable and ambitious, and had lived in Monterrey all of his life. He chuckled and said, "I had no choice, everyone in my family have been bankers for as long as I can remember."

He was twenty one years older than Abby, an Oxford graduate who had never been married. She thought him to be quite elegant and for the remainder of the evening, despite a host of people moving about, they managed to find a quiet niche along the edge of the ballroom where they drank champagne and talked with a kind of openness that suggested the possibility of future plans.

Over the course of the next six months, she and John saw each other as often as they could; he seemed driven by his work and it brought back memories of her father. But in the traditions of Mexico, such dedication went above and beyond criticism. When he proposed she said yes for reasons she wasn't sure of, but it had something to do with stability and comfort.

It was during the bewildering first years of her marriage that she began to adapt, learning to delicately balance her life between her husband's absences and the solitude and peace of the mountains. 'Don't be unhappy, accept things as they are,' she would cry soundlessly, '…don't be unhappy, accept things as they are.' They were words she kept repeating to herself until they became no more than an accumulation of sounds that connected to nothing within her mind.

She simply could not understand John coming home at such odd hours, or his evasive answers when she asked a few innocent questions about his whereabouts. But she told herself that maybe she shouldn't complain until she more fully understood the situation, that she knew little about the world of banking, that it was her duty to believe in him, and that her limited knowledge might cause her to misinterpret his conduct---and in the tortured restlessness of not wanting to conceive of her marriage as having been a mistake, and by some kind of illogical sanction, she absolved him and placed the blame on herself. But there remained within her a dim, persistent certainty which told her that something wasn't right and that the thing she continued to feel was loneliness.

CHAPTER   5

In the sunrise silence of early morning, Matt Callahan stood by the stone fireplace of his cabin, looking at the remnants of last night's fire, checking for hot spots and trying to think of any last minute items he might have forgotten to pack.

Juan was there to say goodbye, giving him a six pack of Coors to make sure, as he put it, he had plenty of gas in his tank. The plan was for Juan to come later, because Matt didn't like leaving the place deserted for any length of time.

"Let me know when you need me," he said. "And be careful, don't drive off one of those mountain roads."

Matt smiled, "Now why would I drive off a mountain?"

And The Mountains Cried

"I don't know, Champ, anything can happen. Personally I don't trust those roads."

"You're too smart, those mountain roads would never fool you."

Juan looked at him with an odd expression. "Sometimes it's the smart ones get caught nappin," he said, "most nearly got me once."

As they walked to Matt's van, Samson, stepping lightly, followed close behind, reaching out at times, nudging Matt's back with his nose. Matt turned and scratched him on his forehead. "Stay in the shadows, big fella," he said. "I don't want you getting yourself shot."

Matt had packed his drawing equipment, including a portable drawing table on one side of his van, and his clothes on the other. He thought it would take a couple of months to complete the plans and told Juan so.

"Good," Juan said, "good, but you don't want to judge it too close, Champ, cause there's always something happens you don't expect."

"Well, we can't know everything."

"Yeah, you're right, Champ, I wouldn't want'a think that what I know is all there is."

Matt smiled and started to pull out some money for any unexpected expenses, but Juan waved it off.

"Anything comes up, I'll take care of it," he said. "You've done plenty for me. And don't worry, I'll be lookin after everything."

Greg Gannaway

"Goodbye, Juan."

"Keep it clean, Champ, don't do nothing I wouldn't do."

Interstate-35 was crowded, lots of big rigs coming out of Laredo. It was always that way, but Matt wasn't pressed and knew that once he reached the other side of San Antonio, there would be less traffic.

For the hundredth time he wished Brandi was still alive. It was trips like this when he missed her the most. She had died two years ago from the crippling effects of old age. He remembered how she looked at the end: her muzzle and eyebrows had turned white and she was unable to stand on her hind legs.

Until the very last, though, this Grande dame of the hill-country was his constant companion, riding everywhere with him. People would pause to say, "What a beautiful golden retriever." Brandi would simper. She knew she was beautiful. When properly groomed, she thought herself to be the queen of Texas.

Three days before her fifteenth birthday she suffered a stroke and the next day it was apparent to Matt that they would never take another trip together again. At the vet he hugged her, hugged her hard, for all the hugs he hadn't given her over the past years.

And The Mountains Cried

Then he turned and fled. He had never realized how much he would miss her until she was gone.

The road ran flat between San Antonio and Laredo, cutting through a badland sprawl of brown pastures; dust devils springing suddenly from the ground in twirling hazes, eating away the earth and disappearing. There was a kind of harsh beauty to the land that appealed to Matt's simple leanings, lots of wild life; it was a part of Texas he had come to like.

He drove past a remote little cemetery; two people, old and bent, were placing flowers on a grave. Matt looked away, as if to shake off the sight and realized that he had never liked cemeteries. They disturbed him in a manner he could not explain. Let others bury their dead, he thought; his body would be cremated and his ashes thrown to the wind.

But on this day dying wasn't on his mind, he felt good; the land stretched away, on either side of the road, into a pale blue sky. The drive seemed easy, as if the van was on automatic pilot and he only sat behind the wheel. It gave him a sense of freedom.

At Pearsall the highway veered west, then swung back south. 'Alonzo's Short Stop' in red letters on a lighted window flashed past. Matt watched the road, driving at an even, safe speed as a matter of habit. There was a railed bridge that crossed a deep ravine and a sign that said DRIVE SAFE. Some unknown soul had punctuated the sign with five clean bullet holes. Matt slowed down, drove slowly, shifting his glance down to the Frio River. This was a sight he did enjoy, turning his head to keep looking at the flowing water as he drove past.

As he gazed down at the river, he caught a flash of something in his rear-view mirror, like chrome catching light out of the sun. He narrowed his eyes and pulled his van along the bridge railing for another look. It was big and black and gleaming---and closing fast. Matt made a friendly attempt to wave, but it seemed to him that his van was almost standing still as the tractor-trailer rumbled passed, a rushing burst of pink-nosed, bawling cattle bound for slaughter.

He waited for the swishing air to settle, then eased his van across the bridge, doubled back down a gravel road and stopped at an overnight camping site along the river. Slowly and peacefully sky and water deepened. Matt pressed his back into the leather seat, his hands resting easy on the steering wheel. Through the foliage of the live oaks he could see the glint of the Frio River. He let his head hang back, feeling his body relax. After a short rest, he started his van, made a wide swing along the river and drove to the highway. Next stop---Mexico.

C H A P T E R   6

It was cloudless and hot on the day Matt Callahan arrived in Monterrey, the blue of the sky soiled by a spread of choking, gassy air hanging motionless above the city. Strapped in by his seatbelt, he leaned forward, placing both hands firmly on the steering wheel, at one with the van, carried forward by a current of trucks, buses and cars of every conceivable year, make and model. Their sight filled the windshield, pressing him on either side. The street had no lanes and vehicles moved in and out like horses on a racetrack. He inhaled the odors of their sooty exhausts and tried to make his way toward the mountains in the distance, but there were few street signs and the map Juan had drawn seemed of little use. His only thought now was to keep from being swallowed up by the grinding motion around him.

"What a mess," he whispered as he steered his van to the outer edge of a wide street, traffic honking and whizzing around him. Then, as if dropped from the sky, there appeared a taxi parked along the side of the street. He looked again; it was true and, with horns blaring from all sides, he managed to pull his van to a stop next to it. The driver stood idly by his cab, bowed by the heat, his eyes lit gently with humor, sensing, with only modest interest, Matt's distress.

"Hola, Senor. You are lost, yes?"

Matt shook his head, took out Juan's map and, speaking in a Spanish dialogue open for criticism, asked for directions to Hotel Chipinque. The driver pushed back his hat and pointed to the mountains stretching along the edge of the city. "There," he said, in a loud tone, "is where you need to go, Senor." And with a slow, dramatic wave of his arm, he motioned for Matt to follow him.

Preparing himself for the worst, Matt kept his eyes fixed on the back of the taxi as they swung into the traffic. But, surprisingly, the driver drove along the side of the road at a slow, even speed that made following easy.

The streets were edged by tight sidewalks. Along the sidewalks were dark shop fronts, blotched and streaked by age. They passed houses, the roof lines slanted, sagging, the color of the walls washed away by the years. A man stood hunched in the hovel, his face gaunt, with staring eyes and sunken features; perhaps

And The Mountains Cried

nothing to mark the passage of his days but the movement of the cars along the street. Matt felt a slight shudder and wondered what error of humanity had brought the man to such a state and suddenly understood the grinding poverty that Juan had always feared.

After several miles, he and the taxi turned south toward the mountains. The street opened over a long bridge crossing a dry river bed. Matt raised his eyes and watched as the mountains loomed closer, rising and dropping without order, a single sculptured form spreading before him like a protective wall.

As he climbed into the twists and turns of an ascending road, the traffic clogged streets of Monterrey vanished behind him. The road narrowed, clinging to the sides of steep ridges, the earth rolling down, dropping away, branches of trees meeting above, streaming across massive stones, shutting out the sun and leaving moments when he was left to drive in the shaded light with no sight of the sky.

He began to feel relaxed in the solitude when, for some unexplainable reason, there came upon him traces of alarm. The skin on his arm would prick up from time to time and there seemed the dim possibility that the even course of his life was, in some vague form, about to change.

High above, the Chipinque Hotel seemed small against the vastness of its setting, stretching in a long, low line across a rocky ledge on the northern face of the Sierra Madre Mountains, its stucco walls glistening white in the pure, high air.

As he approached the hotel, Matt noticed a series of well-tended gardens along either side of the road. The air was fresh, it brought the warm smell of sunshine. He followed the taxi under a wide canopy that covered the main entrance, stopped his van and got out. After paying the taxi driver, he turned and was met by a quiet, courteous older man in a cherry-colored jacket with a mellow face and black hair.

"Buenos dias, senor," he said politely as he ushered Matt into the lobby. "Welcome to the Chipinque Hotel."

The reception desk set under a wide spread of light covering the back wall of a large room. Everyone was efficient, cordial and English speaking, the clerk saying, "Enjoy your stay, Senor," as she handed him his room key.

Matt made his way back across the lobby and stepped out into the clean, high air. He resented the fact that he felt tired, but he never took naps and asked the porter where he could get a cup of coffee.

The porter nodded politely, "Si Senor, I will show you."

He led Matt up a long stone walkway edged by a variety of green plants, orange tipped and yellow blossomed. He thought their rich shades were beautiful, different from that of other plants he'd seen. They were not just color, but seemingly a living form of light, their brightness holding the scented essence of the mountains. The scent filled his nose, lightened him, it was a smell he liked.

"I will take your bags to your room, senor."

Matt thanked the porter and handed him fifty pesos.

The restaurant stood on a knoll separate from the hotel, neatly built, wrapped in long bands of glass overlooking Chipinque Park. It had the precise shape of a square, blending away into the natural reflection of the green ledges rising above it. People were moving in and out, the sound of their voices filling the room. Matt stepped from the sidewalk through the thick oak doors and waited to be seated, watched as a pretty Mexican girl approached him, her steps light as those of a dancer, her skirt swelling slightly as she walked directly to him.

"Good afternoon, Senor," she said, smiling at him gaily with gleaming white teeth and dark eyes. "This way please."

She led him through the crowded dining area, past a flurry of activity from a party sitting at a large table. The women were wearing gently colored lace dresses, sport coats with white carnations for the men. They all seemed elegantly drunk from a long celebration, which even yet seemed not to have ended. The hostess turned to Matt, menu in hand, smiled and, with an inviting gesture of her arm, showed him to a table next to a wide band of windows.

Greg Gannaway

Sunlight fell through the clear glass and he felt the comfort of a black leather chair; it gave the suggestion of luxury and exquisite taste. He ordered coffee and began to enjoy the clean freshness of the heavy white table linens. He was deciding on something to eat, when his glance caught a flash of sun held still on a random pattern of weathered limestone. He thought only of how beautiful the stones looked against the light and of the forms he could have given them. He thought of houses, bare walls of bluish-gray rock rising from the earth.

"Your coffee, Senor," said a youthful voice.

"Oh, yes," he said, returning her a mild glance, "thank you."

He watched the waitress disappear into the crowd and turned his gaze back to the weathered stone, feeling a light running sense of peace with the surroundings, with himself, with the world.

And The Mountains Cried

C H A P T E R   7

It was a little past four in the afternoon. It had turned into one of those beautiful days, rooftops from the city far below gleaming in the sun.

Matt sat at his table, relaxed, gazing into a blue-white sky, clouds clinging to the mountains, soft as cotton. He had not noticed Abby entering the restaurant, but through an odd little fragment of light, caught a glimpse of her figure as she moved through the tightly bunched tables. He turned and watched; she moved closer, becoming more clearly visible as she moved closer still. She turned and looked at Matt on her way to join three ladies at the table next to his. Her eyes went past him without stopping.

Greg Gannaway

There is a moment when a man becomes aware of a woman, not in neighborly friendliness, but as a woman, a being of flesh and beauty and sweetness. It can happen in the flash of a glance, a look, the touch of a hand, the grace of someone's movements. His face tightened and, in that moment, seeing her sitting so close, the thought of never seeing her again crossed his mind, and suddenly he knew that something had opened deep within his consciousness and he saw her as he had never seen another woman.

He sat in a posture of helpless uncertainty, as if she were the only awareness he could now experience, and that he was being held to his seat---or to her---unable to move; an unfamiliar emotion that went beyond the clarity of words, something which he had never felt and could not recognize. He looked again: she had deep brown eyes like her hair, it fell across her shoulders and she wore silver hoops in her ears that flashed in the light like fire on metal. Her face was of such beauty it seemed veiled by the reflection touching her profile, as if a picture taken in soft focus. She was slender and fragile-looking, the essence of feminine simplicity, like a beautiful piece of sculpture reduced to its essential form---and it seemed a discredit to man that such beauty should be subjected to the stress and strains of the outer world. He noticed the long, delicate fingers of her hand resting on the table.

She glanced at him once, but he quickly looked away, trying hard not to stare and told himself to quit

And The Mountains Cried

acting stupid, he'd seen good-looking women before; besides, she probably wasn't even his type, though what was his type he'd never been quite sure. He took a sip of water and wondered why breathing had suddenly become difficult.

Then, in a smooth, even motion, she turned to him and gave him such a look that he almost spilled the glass of water he was holding. But this time he did not turn away and held her glance. She looked at him no longer than the beat of a resting heart, but there seemed a slight shift of expression in her face, as if, in the stillness of that moment, she held his glance just long enough to acknowledge his presence.

A song began to play; it spoke of lost love from far away times. A waiter in a black vest stood beside her table, nodding attentively, as she pointed to an item on the menu. He smiled and wrote down her order.

A succession of minutes passed, time seemed an unyielding reality, enclosing on his every thought. He wanted to say something, to bridge the distance between them, the distance of two people, strangers, on a sun filled day, high in the Sierra Madre Mountains. He felt his lips tighten involuntarily; as if to underscore the passing minutes, the closeness of her presence. How could he reach her…some excuse, any excuse, but what would he say---God, he felt clumsy.

He tried not to look at her; he had to look, afraid she might disappear and he would never see her again. There were moments when he forgot where he was and for what purpose, like the joy of a child held by the sight of something he truly loved.

He watched as she sipped her coffee, her slim body fitting easily to the contours of a cushioned chair. She sat as if concerned with nothing more than the pleasure of being with friends.

In that moment the serenity of his cabin in the woods and the easy ways of life in Texas flashed across his mind. He had his work and there was an occasional woman---why complicate his life, he thought. He had always felt reasonably content and happy; maybe it was best to leave things alone. But something mysterious, beyond all rational consideration, was pushing him forward and he felt himself lean toward her. "I am..." he began, but was never able to finish the sentence. A burst of laughter filled the large table next to them and they both turned to look.

After a moment, he summoned his courage and said, with a flicker of his eyes toward the table of lace dresses and sport coats. "Whatever was said must have been funny."

She ran her finger around the rim of her coffee cup before meeting his gaze, the sound of his voice hanging between them, as if she was contemplating his words and wondering if a response would be proper. Then he saw the trace of a smile on her lips and she turned fully and looked straight at him, a faint radiance in her dark eyes, on her cheeks.

"Yes, it would seem so," she said.

And The Mountains Cried

He felt something jump inside. "I'm sorry to bother you," he said, "but I was hoping you could help me?"

"If I can," she replied.

He tried to smile, his voice rising slightly, feeling the awkwardness of the moment.

"I'm looking for a piece of property here in the mountains. It's close to the Chipinque Hotel…at least I think it is…"

Matt muttered to himself as he fumbled for his map. She waited patiently, letting her eyes move to the surface of the table as he spread the map over the white linen.

She studied it for only a moment and said, "Oh, yes, Carrelera a Chipinque…it is not far from here. I can see it from the terrace of my house."

She hesitated and then suddenly, surprisingly, in defiance of the strict Mexican culture under which she had always lived, heard herself say:

"I was just leaving. If you like, I will show you."

Matt's face quickened with a smile. The voice, the face, the hair, the easy way she turned to meet him, he could feel himself being drawn in.

It is such attractions that allow each generation to revolve, begin again. The way is simple, the power never ending. Matt sensed this, felt its pull in a way that would change him forever.

Abby smiled gaily and told her friends goodbye. Then she turned her eyes to Matt, the straight mass of her brown hair moving in a gentle ripple, like waves in a pond.

"Are you ready?" she asked

Her friends at the table glanced wide eyed at each other and spoke in hurried whispers. Never had they witnessed Abby to make such a rash offer, one making a rather impressive gesture with her arm in the air and, clearing her throat, politely asked, "Abby, are you sure about this?"

There was the half-hint of a smile on Abby's face as she pushed her cup away and rose from the table, a mild, amused expression intended to dismiss the question and divert the situation into a non-issue. She had always been open to trying new things, meeting new people. Still, she was not sure why she had made the offer, but there lay within her something that had separated this moment from the normal, allowing her to breathe in a fresh breath of air.

Abby's eyes moved directly to her friends, then back to Matt. "The gentleman seems quite nice. I will be fine."

She said it quietly, with an odd kind of certainty, her voice soft, distant, as if giving an answer not to her friends, but to a thought of her own.

Matt was slightly surprised by her offer, but felt no need to know the reason and simply nodded his head and smiled. She picked up her check and they walked to the cashier. Matt wanted to pay, but she would not allow it.

And The Mountains Cried

Outside the mountains rose above them, reaching into the clouds, it was pleasantly quiet after the noisy rush of the restaurant. Abby drew it into herself, like a breath.

"Do you come here often?" Matt asked.

She turned to him. "Yes," she said, "as often as I can, but my husband, unfortunately, has never shared my enthusiasm…"

She hesitated for a moment, her voice sliding into the afternoon air. Then, "…I've never understood why he's never come here," she said. "For some reason he doesn't like the mountains." For a moment she came near to unexpected tears, then dashed her hand to her eyes and began to laugh. "Silly of me, and on such a pretty day…" Her long dark lashes flickered in the sunlight. She almost cried again.

Matt let the moment pass before speaking. "I've never been here," he said, "it's nice and cool. Austin's like a furnace this time of year."

"Oh, you are from Austin, Texas?"

"Yes, I'm sorry, my name is Matt Callahan."

"I am Abigail Margarita Casal," she said smiling, "but my friends call me Abby."

When she spoke there came the hint of her Spanish blood, the voice of a woman looking out over blue seas into untouched distances, waiting for a love that was yet to come.

"Abby," he said, "that's a nice name."

Greg Gannaway

He reached in his wallet and handed her a business card: **Matt Callahan-Architect/Developer.**

"A friend of mine owns the land I spoke of. It's been in his family for years...wants me to take a look."

"Oh, really," she said, pointing. "I think we need to go this way."

Then with eyes narrowed against the brightness of the sun, she turned to Matt Callahan, keeping a bit of distance between them, as if seeing him for the first time. She was looking at a man whom she had only just met. What she saw was the easy, casual figure of a man from Texas. She noticed his athletic bearing and the effortless way he moved---a tall body in simple clothes, a white sport shirt, light pants, a slim waist and loose blond hair made to shine in the sun.

They walked slowly down the sunny sidewalk, nodding to various passing strangers. She watched, only slightly surprised, as Matt placed several pesos into a tin cup, giving a glimmer of hope to the gnawing drabness of a homeless man on his shredded blanket.

"That's old Joe," she said. "He once worked here, but his mind began to fail him a while back. Each year he seems to be getting a little worse. There have been orders all around that he is the only beggar to be allowed on the grounds. It is nice of you to help him."

They were talking normally, casually, without strain, as if they had forgotten the purpose of their being together. It had been a pleasant meeting and she wished it could go on longer. Then it occurred to her that she might never see him again, that this might be their only moment in the great sweep of things. She could not give any reason for the thought, yet she wondered of this man from Texas, heard the whispers of old dreams and felt good that they were walking together in the high mountain air of Chipinque Park.

"Here I am," she said, touching his arm, "this is my car."

Matt turned and spotted his van. "I'm just across the way. I'll follow you."

He swung in behind her as she drove out of the parking lot, into the coils of a descending mountain road. The pavement shrank to a narrow lane between ancient live oaks, their twisting trunks pressing close, like a row of sentinels, swallowing the road in huge dark shadows. Several turns and a few minutes later took them only a short distance from the Chipinque Hotel. There were no signs; it seemed the road was rarely used, nothing to break the silence and stillness but random wedges of sunlight cutting through the forest.

He saw her pull along the side of the road and come to a slow stop. She opened her car door, put her feet on the pavement and got out of the car, then turned and watched as he slung his camera and a large satchel over his shoulder, shut his car door and walked to meet her.

"Well, this is it," she said. "What do you think?" Then, leaning her head far back, she shaded her eyes, as if searching the sky and pointed upward, high into the green mountains, at a white house jutting from the edge of a sheer rock cliff. "That's my house up there."

"That must be some view."

"Yes, I can see all of Monterrey."

As they stood along the edge of the road, Matt's eyes stopped just beneath the branches of a live oak. In its shadow was a crumbling stone structure rising off-plumb in collapsing angles, with only a partial roof. From the survey, Matt recognized it to be Juan's family home. He wondered of the life and memories that had been breathed into the walls of the old house, felt its warmth and thought of the many feet that had passed over the threshold and trod the wide pine floors, now old and creaking from age.

The property was bordered on three sides by wooded park land. Sunlight fell like golden dust through the trees, struck the ground in sprawling patches of light and dark, their shapes forming and disappearing and forming again in shadowy patterns of leaf and limb, rock and grass. From the rear came the sound of water splashing and slapping through heavy boulders, a light roll of mist cooling the September air.

Matt Callahan smiled, then looked at her and said, "Walk with me."

It was she who took his arm as they moved down the slope, then dropped it as they reached the ruins of the old stone house. The gesture had been automatic, she had not noticed it and suddenly she was aware that they were alone; an awareness that seemed to stress the fact that they had only just met. But she allowed it no further implication and leaned back, just enough to feel the faint shift of a breeze in her hair, conscious of nothing but the man by whom she was standing.

He glanced at her hesitantly, feeling a bit of tightness in his throat and said, "Abby, I need to check out a few things...it won't take long. If you have time, I'd like to buy you a cold drink when I'm finished?"

It was the muscles of her face that made Abby realize the nature of her reaction to his question. She did not speak; she only looked at him, her vision stretched across the silence. Then she dropped her head, closing her eyes, acknowledging to herself the times when she had thought of meeting someone like Matt Callahan: when standing alone on the terrace of her mountain home, in the silence of a sleepless night; she had thrown the idea aside, not wanting to hold the thought inside her mind, not wanting to know that somewhere deep down she truly wished it to happen. She would feel a stab of guilt, the emotions of her mind fighting the thought---a stab like something pulling her to a place she dare not go.

When she raised her head, Matt saw the look of uncertainty in her face, the look of a thousand thoughts rushing to fight an indefensible desire, and in that silent instant, against every doubt and warning in her mind, he heard her whisper, "I think I would like that." And with one simple move, she slipped down to sit on one of the low rock window ledges of the old house. The stone was worn smooth and she felt its warmth seeping through her skirt into her skin.

She watched his figure move among the trees; saw the lightness in his steps, smooth and fluid. He seemed to blend with the setting, as if belonging to the countryside. It was becoming to him.

From his leather case he took out the survey drawing Juan had given him, unfolded it and made his way to the back of the property. He stopped just as he reached the edge of the creek, turned and began moving from one side of the property to the other. He would stand for a moment, then gently grasp his pencil between his fingers and extend his arm out straight, holding the pencil parallel with his eyes, allowing for a quick read of the slope and drainage of the property. As he moved forward he would repeat the process, taking keen notice of each tree. Later he would mark the ones he wanted to save with bright pink survey ribbon. It was a process he had done many times before.

In the narrow space between the silhouettes of two trees, she saw him drop down into a squatting position and begin to draw, his pencil moving freely over a sketch pad. When finished he did a quick examination of the work, then stood erect, waved and walked toward her in the tall grass.

"It's a nice piece of property…much better than I expected."

And The Mountains Cried

Abby nodded, "Yes, it is…"

He turned to her and held out the sketch he had drawn. It was of the crumbling stone building, done with the clean, sharp strokes of his pencil. In the right hand corner it said: *To Abby, a beautiful lady…*

"Thanks for showing me the way," he said.

She held the picture at arm's length and again felt something stir within her.

"It's really beautiful, how could you do it so quickly?"

"It's a hobby…and I use it in my work." Then he smiled and said, "I like your accent."

Her eyes stirred. "Spanish blood, no French, no German, no Scotch or Irish, not even Mexican. My family seemed not to have married carelessly."

As they began to walk to the road, she felt his hand touching her elbow. The effort seemed not to be one of simple courtesy, as a man might help a woman up a sloping ridge, but of affection, as if the light touch of hidden attraction. At that moment, something rose within her, not a thought or a feeling, but a wave of physical desire.

On the slopes around them, the broad spread of the oak trees stood like twisted forms of sculpture, immovable, gnarled in masculine simplicity. Sun rays fell through the leaves, sweeping the ground, their faces.

She looked at him, feeling strange, unraveled, as if she had been caught, and that he knew what she was feeling. She hadn't expected this to happen and, for a moment, she wanted to turn and run…somewhere, anywhere. She hadn't come here for this and wondered if she had already gone too far, that maybe she was getting into something that wasn't as harmless as it first appeared, and that maybe she should leave.

But her eyes kept coming back to his face and the world seemed to grow misty and unreal, light spreading gently around them, the little flash of her earrings in the sun, the sound of the creek moving, forms seen for a moment and then gone…as if in a dream and yet awake, rising within her, in soft, clear whispers, something deep and old, drawing her in and she knew she could not leave.

The sound of her voice seemed no louder than the rhythm of her breath, as if coming from somewhere among the leaves when she asked, "Would you like to come to my house for some ice tea…it's only a few minutes away."

Again, Matt was surprised, but took little time to answer. "Yes, I'd like that." he said.

From the road a high stone wall rose in a continual vertical line that cut the house and garden from the street. They entered through a brown gate made of huge oak planks, banded together with straps of iron and held upright by massive hinges. The brown paint had begun to wear off in crumbling patches. Matt heard the heavy gate creak to a close behind them and suddenly felt the intimacy of his surroundings.

And The Mountains Cried

"This is beautiful," he said.

"It's one of my favorite parts of the house."

Green ferns hung in clusters from the twisting branches of the trees, their leafy limbs cooling the garden with wide areas of shade. They walked past a small stone bench, down a footpath winding through quiet pools of water. Long, delicate stems lined the edges of the water, extending themselves in graceful swoops over the ponds, ending in colorful flowers. The water reflected the flowers as if they were brightly colored rocks and the fragrance in the air seemed to come not from the flowers, but from the colors dancing beneath the water.

There was a jingle of keys as they stepped up onto the entry porch. Abby slipped one of the keys into the door and pushed it open.

Matt felt a rush of cool air, stepped inside and stood at the edge of the living room as Abby closed the door. His gaze moved about slowly. He noticed there was no ornamentation, no tightly confined spaces, only vast windows throwing the space open to the sun, the trees, to the city beyond, as if each element was part of the room's completion. Canvases by the great masters of Mexico hung along the walls in an explosion of color. Brilliant rugs were scattered across polished tile floors. The furnishings were simple: long, low couches with clean lines and deep cushions, highlighted in shades of green and orange and red and yellow. This was Abby's concept of wealth, he thought, the wealth of selection, not of accumulation.

He spoke not a word, but his approval was expressed in the features of his face. He felt at peace, relaxed in the serene comfort of the room, his breath coming easy and, from some remote source, came a feeling that he belonged here.

After a moment she heard him say in a low tone, a tone of admiration. "Nice place."

Abby led the way and offered him a seat on the couch. Josie appeared at the same moment, showing neither surprise or any other emotion at the presence of Abby's guest.

"Can I get you anything, Mrs. Abby?"

"Yes, Josie, please, ice tea."

As she spoke she turned to Matt, smiling, a bright and easy look on her face.

"Matt, excuse me for a minute," she said, glancing at his sketch, then back at him. "I won't be long."

Matt sat deep in the couch, not moving, except for the fingers of one hand sliding along the side of his cheek. He watched her as she crossed the length of floor between them, making a quick study of the graceful sway of her hips. She seemed to be of no particular age, or that age between ages when it was difficult to say just what age she really was. But he guessed her to be around thirty-nine or forty and, with reasonable certainty, estimated her height at about five foot six.

And The Mountains Cried

Through the span of silence he wondered, as he had in the restaurant, about her husband. She had mentioned him only once, not in a personal way, but simply to say that he was a banker. Having never met the man, Matt could not understand the slight dislike that had formed in his mind. He tried to rationalize his feelings, after all the guy was a banker---who liked bankers? But, of course, that had little to do with it. This guy was Abby's husband and he could feel a twinge of envy as he wondered of their life together.

He looked about the room, his glance stopping on the row of abstract paintings hanging on the wall. They made the room seem larger, the wall brighter, and he wondered whether the artists were all from Mexico or from other countries and were they pure oils and what a nice arrangement of shapes and colors. Then it struck him, the shock of the unexpected. He tried to stop it, but the thought burst upon him involuntarily, beyond his defenses, closing his mind to all reason. He could not explain it---he did not care, he knew only that wherever she had been before this moment, that in some way and for whatever reason, she now belonged with him.

He sank deeper into the couch, feeling a dim, unsteady hope which he had never felt before; the hope that they would somehow be together always.

Abby returned and, tilting her head slightly, smiled, as she held his sketch out for him to see. She had hastily mounted it in a sterling silver frame.

As she sat down, she turned the picture and looked at it for a long time, a thin edge of light outlining the silver frame. She read the words: *To Abby, a beautiful Lady*, as if she had received something more than just the picture and wondered, oddly, of his feelings when he wrote her name.

"It's funny," she said, almost in a whisper, "it's like seeing something I've never seen, yet somehow remembering it…" She turned her face to his. "I suppose that sounds a little strange…"

It was getting late in the afternoon, the sun sinking, holding the room in a shadow of unmoving light. Her gaze seemed to move past Matt, through the shadows themselves, into some other time, some other place…far away.

"Will that be all Mrs. Abby?"

"Oh, yes, Josie…thank you."

Abby leaned forward and with one hand flat against the polished marble coffee table, poured the tea from a simple crystal container, feeling a small twitch from somewhere inside, knowing he was watching as she placed ice cubes into the glasses.

"Sugar or lemon?"

"Yes, both please."

She felt the touch of his fingertips as she passed him the glass. "Your business card says you're an architect and also a developer. How does that work?"

Matt sat silently for a moment, the line of his sight looking out through the wide windows to a spread of oak trees clinging to the mountain slopes. It all seemed beautiful to him; natures magnificence, here in the quiet grandeur of the Sierra Madres Mountains.

"I create places," he said, turning to her. "I'll locate a piece of ground and ask myself: What can I do here? And the moment I ask that, it seems I've got to do it. I like to think of it as giving life to empty spaces."

She wondered why he seemed to be watching her face so intently. "Will what you do here blend with the neighborhood?" she asked.

He smiled, then his face slipped slowly into earnestness, as if seeing through his own eyes an image of what was yet to be built.

"It will." He spoke the words simply, not as a boast, but as a personal guarantee of the exacting values of his work. "I like my buildings to belong exactly where you see them standing, as a compliment to the landscape instead of a disgrace---and to enhance the character and existence of those who live in and around them. It's the only way I know."

Abby felt within herself the sincerity of his answer. Smiling, she extended her glass out to touch his.

"Salud."

"Salud."

As she lowered her glass she noticed his eyes still watching her, not moving, as if something still hung between them, something unsaid, unnamed, sitting there in the room with them, like a dark shadow---and that he wanted her to know of it. There was a moment's pause; Matt saw her looking straight at him, as if in some special awareness of his presence; he felt the effort of her glance, searching, but he did not recognize it as effort, only as understanding. He felt himself supported by the glance and, in the silence of that one moment, understood the peacefulness of his feelings: that he felt no sense of pressure, no need to hide the phobic struggles he had experienced in the past, struggles that seemed to mysteriously vanish whenever he was with her.

Abby sipped her tea and gently pressed a napkin to her lips. There seemed a delicate flow in the room, as if the coolness of the air held them together, and the air that touched him carried his touch to her. It was nothing he had told her in words, but there was no denying that, in that moment, something had passed between them. Her glance said simply that somehow, in her own way, she now had an understanding of what he wanted her to know and nothing was needed to state it; that maybe she had been aware of it even before he came to her, and more: that she was completely untroubled by the knowledge. She did not know why she felt certain of being the only person to know of his anxieties, but she looked upon it as a special kind of gift.

When Matt turned to her, there was an undisguised purposefulness in the expression of his face. It made her think of her first trip up into the mountains, of looking into a blue, sun-filled sky and feeling a sense

of peace and promise; it was as if she heard him say:
"I'm glad you know, Abby."

But why, he wondered, didn't he feel it here. This
was the very kind of situation he had always tried to
avoid; yet here, with her, in this room, he felt only
relief, an unfamiliar relief that spread through his body,
flowing like water, washing everything away, the pain,
the anxiety, the fear---all disappeared. He did not know
why, because never had he been able to comprehend
the process of his anxiety. It was like a current flowing
through his body, muscles coiled around one another,
pulled taut, his breath becoming short and shallow, a
mysterious inner threat made more terrible by feelings
of shame and guilt; that it came with a fright he had
never before known, and that on a rainy afternoon in
Texas, sitting at a table having thanksgiving dinner
with the parents' of an old girlfriend, it came.

Why he suddenly recalled the incident, he did not
know; it hit him in a flash, his head jerking, as if
awakened by the sound of an alarm.

It seemed everything was fairly normal on that day,
only he couldn't follow a single word anyone was
saying. He was distracted by the voices of everyone at
the table, as if they were all talking at once.
Inexplicably he felt seized, unable to move, held in a
realm of something ominous, dark, that had no form.
He began to tremble with fear. As the minutes ticked
by, he tried to compose himself, but the effort was
futile and he began to feel dizzy.

"Is anything wrong?" his girlfriend asked. But he was unable to answer or even look up, the muscles in his neck drawn tight. He put his hands together, trying to keep them from shaking, but still they shook. The more he tried to hide his fear, the more it showed. He could feel something breaking loose inside. He wanted to creep away, hide and wondered if he had suddenly cracked. Why was this happening to him? He did not know.

Distraught, he mumbled some vague words and made his way to the safety of the bathroom. Grateful to have found refuge, he sat huddled in silence on the toilet seat, hands gathered in his lap, the back of one hand clasp tight in the palm of the other, as if trying to squeeze away the fear he did not understand. It was quiet there, and he began to relax. Finally he told himself that he would have to go out and explain to everyone what was going on. But how could he explain? He didn't know himself.

During the drive home he remembered the rain trickling down the windshield, wiper blades pushing it aside. His girlfriend, desperate to understand, repeatedly asked him what was wrong. He took a long, deep breath, inhaling the damp air, letting it out slowly, very slowly, wanting to explain, to justify, to clarify his behavior. But he had no explanation to give her. How could he be afraid of nothing at all? Why was he still shaking inside? "That was not really me," he replied in a low voice. But in the end, the words were not convincing and he could tell by the look on her face that their relationship was over.

Abby looked at him, her face revealing the concern she was feeling. "Matt, are you okay?" she asked softly.

There was an orange glow in the late afternoon sky, it fell across the roof of Abby's mountain home, through the glass doors, hit the wall behind Matt's couch. The glow moved gently across his forehead and, in that moment, he felt the burden of his apprehensions fall away.

He smiled. "I'm fine, Abby," And she saw in his eyes the hint of lighthearted pleasure. There was the tinkling of ice as his fingers closed firmly about the glass, his arm steady. He felt at ease. He felt at home.

"What about you," he asked, "how's life in Monterrey?"

There was a faint tightening of her lips, the question hung in her mind, an unanswered emptiness that she had never been able to fill. Her stock answer was always, 'Oh, just fine, the people are nice and there are many things to do and see.' But now the question seemed difficult and she wondered why his presence made her want to confess things that were not fully confessed in her own mind: that feeling of separation between her way of living and the life of which she had dreamed.

"More lemon or sugar...?"

"A little more lemon...thanks."

She sat for a long moment, a shaft of light bouncing off the surface of her glass. Then she raised her eyes and smiled. There was a trace of sadness in the smile.

"Well, I suppose I should be happy. I have my friends there, and living downtown has its advantages, but my feelings for Monterrey only reach to a certain point and then they seem to stop." She hesitated, pondering her next words. "…It's hard for me to explain…it's like I'm sitting in a small boat in a long stretch of water and the shore is just before me. But, as I start to row toward it, I get caught in the tide and can never get there. It frightens me."

Matt held his silence, watching her. After a few moments had passed, he asked, "What is it that frightens you, Abby?"

She shook her head and sighed deeply. "I'm not sure…maybe it's the same for everyone…of being left exposed and unprotected, of feeling alone. I…"

She paused for a moment and turned to Matt. The startling clear blue color of his eyes was calm and she knew that he understood, and that she could speak to him as she had not spoken to anyone else.

"…I only know it's not the life I dreamed of when I was young."

It was a side of her she had always kept hidden, neatly folded away, so as not to disrupt the well-conceived life her husband had laid out for her in Monterrey. But the feelings had always been there and now she had acknowledged them to a man from Texas.

For a long moment, Matt simply looked at her, reading her, seeing all the hope and desire that filled her eyes. It's true, he thought: we are always running or hoping or searching---whatever it is we do, one or the other. We long for that world closest to our hearts and keep wondering where is it.

Now, as he looked at her, it was as if he were suddenly seeing her for the first time, as an actual being, in her own space and time, something deeper than looks, a solitary being in a world of lost hearts, whom somehow, across all space, for a moment at least, he had touched…and who had touched him.

He felt surprised. As a rule, he was not one to form close relationships. Since his divorce, he had moved along pretty much by himself. That was all well and good, but then again, he hadn't expected too much. Now to feel the deep presence of someone else pleased and startled him.

Matt cleared his throat. "There are many ways to reach your dreams, Abby," he said presently. "I like to think that no dream can ever be completely lost…just remember they hold all possibilities and are the magic of your life. Keep rowing, you'll find them."

Abby nodded, she was like an artist dancing along the edges, feeling a stab of sorrow at the thought of their time together being almost over. She had come this far, why not test her limits.

"Do you have any plans for dinner?" she asked hesitantly. "Josie's off for the evening, but I think I can put something together."

She caught the flicker of a smile on his face.

"I'd love to," he said. "Will I have time to go to the site?"

"Sure, no hurry, I'll get things started while you're gone."

She followed him to the door, watched as he stepped off the porch and stood for a moment, shading his eyes, taking in the smells and beauty of the garden. Then he settled his vision along the stone path, waving as he made his way to his van; the heavy wooden gate closing behind him with sound of a bank vault.

Abby closed the door, turned and looked across the room. There was a tingling at the very center of her being; it rippled out in tiny waves to her fingertips and she felt as if something was quietly taking over her body. Things suddenly seemed different, it was not the room she had left a few minutes since, and the furniture did not seem the same, but furniture from another time. She opened the sliding glass door and stepped out onto the patio. The sun was sinking lower and lower, the wind whispered in the trees, yellow shafts of light fell across the stone terrace. She looked beyond the terrace, to the city below, but it was not the view she remembered.

And The Mountains Cried

Leaves trembled in the late sun, their edges the color of rusted metal streaming from the trees. She closed her eyes and, in the stillness of that one brief moment, the lost dreams of a little girl from Guadalajara seemed to have once again come alive.

CHAPTER 8

Upstairs a wall of glass ran the length of Abby's bedroom, an invisible barrier between the terrace, the green mountains, and the city below. She stood very still, looking, her eyes traveling out into the hazy shadows of the twilight, not quite believing what she was feeling, as if she had almost lost the ability to think of life as she had once dreamed and was suddenly surprised to discover that it had once again taken over her world.

After taking a quick shower she dried herself with a huge towel that swallowed her body. Standing in the middle of her closet, she tried to decide what to wear. She didn't want to overdress. Maybe her beige slacks with a white blouse and flats...but where were they? Things seemed to have a will of their own in this closet and hid where they liked. Moving about in a rush, she told herself to be calm.

And The Mountains Cried

The September sun was half way down the sky when Matt arrived at the site. It threw long, hot streaks across the grassy ridges. He parked his dodge van on the side of the road, got out and walked through the trees, down the slope of the five acre site until he reached the ruins of Juan's old home. For a long while he stood with legs planted wide apart, his back against the slanting light, studying the general grade of the land, how the late evening sun fell across it, how it drained. It felt good to be out under the open sky and breathe the mountain air. Unconsciously his hand reached out, running over the weathered stones of the old house. One of the stones broke loose, it bounced down the grassy incline into the stream, soft drops of sound rolling through the summer air.

In that moment, in the half-light of the evening, Matt felt something shift inside. Suddenly, without willing it, his reason for being in Monterrey began to fade, no longer was he thinking of the work before him, but of a beautiful face with dark eyes and lustrous brown hair. The desire to see her was intense. He tried to think of why he had come to the site, of the houses, their placement, but her image remained, rising before him, harmoniously shaped and sweetly rounded.

The sun had begun to pale away below the mountains, the twilight settling peacefully across the evening air. Matt shook his head, smiled, and walked quickly up the slope to his van.

When Abby opened the door, she was wearing a flowered apron, her face slightly flushed from the heat of the stove. She held a wooden spoon in her hand.

He looked at her with a hint of shyness in his face. "It got dark before I realized it," he said. "Hope I'm not late."

"Oh, no, not at all…I'm trying something new," she announced triumphantly, as she showed him to the couch. Matt sat down, relaxing into an easy posture, feeling the warmth of the room, letting his back press into the cushions, enjoying the decor and the views that went on forever. The truth was he often felt amazed and surprised. Despite perpetually guarding against walking into a phobic trap, never did he feel that the problem fit him. He didn't over restrict himself because of his anxiety. He lived fully, having accepted its existence so completely that, at times, he barely knew it was with him. It had, in the course of living, settled itself so slowly and deeply and secretly, that there were times when he wondered why he was ever distressed by it. He was able to cope with normal nervousness as the next person. He knew what it was to be anxious before playing in a sporting event, giving a talk, meeting with a potential client about a job, or anticipating a painful confrontation with someone. He knew what it was to take a deep breath before such occasions and face them. But after many years of effort he had not conquered his phobic fear. It was like a burning in his soul---and the vexing question remained: why didn't he feel it here. He let his hand reach out to feel the texture of a small throw pillow, just to convince himself that he could.

Abby turned the radio dial until she found some old American favorites. She set the volume low and ask if he would like something to drink. He met her eyes and smiled---in relief, in deliverance, in laughing astonishment of his anguish, as if it had suddenly all become nothing more than times forgotten.

"A beer, if you have one."

She went to the kitchen and returned, placing two cold mugs of beer on the heavy marble top. She closed her fingers around the handle of her mug and watched Matt take his and, for an instant, wondered if he felt the same crisp coolness as she did and thought how simple it was, how unastonishing. He had been here always. She saw him now as she had seen him when she was a child, an unbroken reflection of past dreams and knew it had to come like this, knowing she had been waiting in this place, for this time.

"I feel as if I've known you all my life." She spoke the words with exquisite gentleness.

She saw his surprised glance, his face held in a question. "But how could that be poss…?" He was unable to complete the sentence, his words flickered, quietly they fluttered and dwindled, and for a moment they looked at each other across a space of more than air, as if searching for what they could not see and what might have been. In his confusion, Matt could only ask: "Have I known you too?"

She looked at him quietly and he saw in her eyes the answer; an answer lifted from some guarded place within her. "Always," she said.

They sat silently before each other for a moment. She saw a faint movement she had noticed to be typical of him, the movement of his finely-shaped mouth curving into the hint of a smile. He let the moment pass, as if to underscore his thoughts. How could he question her, how could he doubt her words? He couldn't, not in this moment, not when there was no weight of panic in him, no fear, no anxiety. This was a time not to be questioned and he knew he had found it here; a strange sense of peace rising through his body, peace he had been unable to find in times past---this room and the shimmering night sky and...

He raised his mug. In the glint of his blue eyes was a smile. "To the green mountains of Chipinque Park and the lady I've known forever."

Abby smiled back and raised her mug with a quiet kind of incredulous wonder, as if some external power had seized her and she was being carried along, unresisting, to a place she had never been. A thought came from some faint beat in her mind and she wondered if it were all true: a toast on a cool summer night, dinner with a man from Texas, the picture he had drawn for her…and chilled foam spilling over two cold mugs of beer. How had this happened?

There had been times in the past when, on special occasions, she had shared a drink with John, hoping to ignite some small spark of romance into their structured lives. It hadn't happened, it had never happened. But on this night the beer tasted wonderful. It seemed almost too much for her to believe. It was a moment to be saved, perhaps forever.

Abby motioned toward the kitchen.

"I won't be long," she said smiling.

He looked up as she walked past him. "Need any help?"

She shook her head, feeling his eyes on her, wondering if he watched her walk away, thinking he might.

He did watch, watched as she walked across the tile floor, passed the massive glass wall, with the silver lights of the city trembling in its blackness. There was a quality of simple elegance in her movement and the fact that she had been able to be human and honest about her feelings made him want to know more. He watched her moving about the kitchen and began to wonder of other things he sensed in her.

She glanced back at him and motioned to the bar. "Why don't you bring our beer and keep me company while I finish up."

Matt walked across the room to the kitchen, placed the mugs on the bar and climbed onto a brightly colored stool. "How's this?"

"Fine," she said, not knowing why her voice dropped toward a whisper. And in the brief space of that moment, she felt her heart contract in a kind of shifting fear, and at the same time with delight. Who are you, she thought, and what has brought you here to me?

She drew a deep breath, feeling a slight tremble in her hand.

"Like another beer?" she asked.

Matt said he would like that and she opened two more, poured them into fresh mugs from the freezer and placed the used ones in the sink.

"How long do you think you'll be here?" she asked, glancing down into the pot of beans she was stirring.

"I'm not sure. Guess it depends on how things go with the houses...first thing I need is a survey crew...know any good ones?"

"I wouldn't know about that, but I could call around." She turned to him, her voice becoming urgent, ragged. "I just...I just hope you don't run into trouble."

"What trouble?"

"Oh, I don't know...the way things are nowadays with the building inspectors, anything might happen."

"What trouble do you mean?"

And The Mountains Cried

Abby stood looking at him, her fingers closed about the wooden spoon. "Texans aren't too popular down here."

"I've never had any complaints."

"That's not what I mean, these guys are greedy, they'll drain you of every penny you have."

"All I want to do is design the houses," he said…and he thought that was all; he would have sworn that was all he wanted, but now his eyes never left the woman standing before him.

She asked about the project and he told her about Juan and why he wanted to build the houses.

"Are you staying at the Chipinque Hotel?" she asked.

His hand moved down the cold wetness of his mug. "Checked in this afternoon. I didn't know there would be such a place in Monterrey."

"It's my favorite. I like being away from everything. No one I know ever comes up here…" She laughed and shook her head. "Well, today was an exception, I invited them."

"And thanks for inviting me. I don't think I've told you, but I'm pretty good at cooking beans."

She looked at him and smiled. "Holding out on me, huh…" She held out the spoon and he climbed down from his stool and moved around the bar into the kitchen. Standing next to her, he removed the lid from the pot and peered into the bubbling water, eyes squinted, nose wrinkled to avoid the steam as he stirred.

"Good job," she said, still smiling.

It was strange to feel so pure a joy in preparing a meal. She had never thought that grating cheese could be so sensual and, for the flash of that one instant, it startled her that she should feel a sudden twinge of guilt. She hadn't done anything, nothing at all, yet the guilt was there. She told herself that they were simply preparing dinner, but that wasn't the whole truth, and she knew it.

She hesitated, not wanting to dwell on the feeling.

"Your pencil drawing is beautiful. Have you ever tried other mediums?"

"My ex-wife got me into oils. I think I've tried them all, but mostly I do watercolors and pencil."

The mention of his ex-wife gave her a twinge of what she did not want to admit was jealousy. She asked: "You're not married?"

"Oh, no, that's been over quite a while. I can't put my finger on it, but in a way I blame myself for what happened. She moved to New York and wanted me to come with her. 'You'll love New York,' she told me, but I liked being in the country and told her I'd love it better from where I was."

He paused, slowly stirring the beans. She saw something had reached him; she couldn't tell whether it was regret or relief.

And The Mountains Cried

"But it wasn't just being in the country that was wrong. There were spaces between us that we were never quite able to close. I don't remember any particular anger. Mostly it was disappointment and, in the end, we figured it was for the best."

She listened, without speaking. After a moment she asked, "Do you ever hear from her?"

"For a while, after the divorce, we talked on the phone, but it's been a long time since I last heard from her."

The answer seemed an end to the subject and Abby did not push for more, but in an awkward, almost selfish way, she found comfort in his answer. She gave him a gentle glance, slid a tray of enchiladas into the oven and set the timer.

"We can take our drinks and sit outside if you like."

Matt gave the beans another stir and followed her through the glass doors into the soft lights of the terrace, the tile floor still warm from the afternoon sun.

From the terrace they could see the city of Monterrey far below. It was of its own world, a great sweep of lights flaring in the darkness. Buildings rose like black shadows, their outlines soft against the night sky. The sky lay against the rim of the city, one pushing against the other, immovable. The city was of what man had conceived. It held a promise for all those who dreamed, and within those dreams came the answers.

Abby Casal let her head fall back and stared up into the sky, seeing the darkness between the stars, those holes in time---and from her heart flowed feelings of which she had almost forgotten. She turned to Matt and saw only his eyes and that he was smiling.

She heard him say: "In Texas views like this come with a high price."

She saw him smile further when she ask: "Will the houses you're designing here have views?"

"They will," he said, "the site demands it."

"All of them?...that'll be quite a challenge won't it?"

There was no sound of effort in his answer. He told her how he wanted the houses to seem as if grown from the earth, each structure an integrated part of the next, whole and complete, as if the site had no other reason for its existence.

Lights flashed in unrestrained tremors across the city. Abby leaned forward, unconscious of her movements. "You must like working with people," she said.

He looked out across the terrace, to the city below. The whole world seemed bathed in a clean, peaceful light, and from the stillness came thoughts of yet more distant things. Beyond the horizon of the city there seemed something else; a life untouched, untroubled, without panic, and he could feel it moving toward him.

And The Mountains Cried

He turned to Abby and when he spoke, his voice was steady and clear.

"Without people," he said, "there's no work, no clients, so I'm glad when people find a better way of living from something I've designed; but I work best alone. I've never cared very much for the opinion of others, I want buildings built exactly as I design them."

The quality of his voice seemed to underline his words, his passion. She watched him, half turned to her, his head lifted. There was no boasting, no flaunting his talents, he conveyed none of these things; he conveyed only a quality exceptional to its basic core: a sense of himself.

"I would never allow my work to be altered by a vision not my own. If it's right and good and if it's sound, then the client will be happy. If not, then I have only myself to blame, no one else. That's the way I work...that's who I am."

Abby sat listening quietly to this man from Texas. She noticed his fingers pressing absently along the arm of his chair as he spoke, as if his hand was moving over the steel beam of a building. There was an instinctive response in his eyes.

He told her how the large residential development firms had their own way of doing things, that their work was done by committees and collaboration, of how they placed public preferences on a chart and designed to satisfy those tastes; cookie cutter designs done for mass markets, monuments to the power of money, greed and all of the fame and honor that society might wish to give.

"That's their choice," he said, "not mine."

She rose from her chair and walked to the stone railing and looked down into the darkness. "Do you realize that your project will be built below my house. It's a long way down, but once it's finished I'll be able to see it from my patio and it will become part of my world." She turned to him and said, "I will think of you each time I see it."

It was the tone of her voice more than the words that made him rise from his chair. She watched him walk toward her, the sound of each step rolling into the night air, bringing him closer, as if filling the space of a lifetime. She stood leaning back against the railing, arms at her side, palms flat against the stone, sensing the twilight world of childhood dreams closing in around her.

He stopped before her. The moonlight seemed to drain sound and, for a long moment, they stood still with the night, lost in a sort of dream, an enchantment beyond time or change. Then he turned away and the moment was gone. Abby felt herself exhale, feeling a twinge of relief, not knowing or understanding why she felt it. She hadn't realized that she had been holding her breath.

She straightened herself and stepped away from the railing. "Would you excuse me, Matt," she said,

And The Mountains Cried

"I'll only be a minute." Her voice was strangely soft, as if not quite ready to pronounce the words she spoke.

Matt walked back to his chair and sat down, feeling suddenly unsettled. Leaning back, he looked up into the night sky, taking a deep breath of the high air, trying to recapture the safety of his own world. He had seen her standing before him in the soft glow of the terrace lights, her body alive, motionless, so still it seemed to tremble; an involuntary, physical sensation hinting at surrender.

Abby returned holding a cold mug of beer in each hand. She sat them on the small iron stand between them. Matt took a long gulp, feeling certain of nothing, yet glad for the gift of his existence.

CHAPTER 9

The moon rose, white and round, just over the naked mass of mountains above Chipinque Park. A slight breeze had risen from the Southeast and they could feel it's cool relief brush their faces. She looked at Matt Callahan. She saw streaks of gray in his blonde hair ruffling in the light wind. It gave him an air of grace and cleanliness, like his crisp white shirt against the night sky and again she wondered how fate had placed this man, who had come so far, on her patio. They had been strangers only a short while ago, but the strangeness of their meeting was now fading; they were alone, no swirling crowds, together on the patio, their existence untouched by the eyes of others, their words heard only by them. She thought of the things they might have become to each other had they met at an earlier time and, in that moment, she imagined the kind of life that might have been hers, the kind of life of which she had always dreamed, and knew that nothing more was needed to complete the night.

Matt leaned back in his chair, shoulders relaxed, his hand closed around the handle of his beer mug. "I've never been to Guadalajara. Didn't you say that's where you were born?"

A sweep of her brown hair fell past the line of her shoulders as she told him of her childhood days on her father's hacienda, how it had been given to her father by her grandfather, as his father had given it to him; that it had been in their family for over a hundred years and was the only hacienda that the legendary leader, Emiliano Zapata, had not taken from them during the Mexican Revolution. She remembered her grandfather once remarking how he purely hated Zapata, but later confessed that he understood his anger and why the people of Mexico had revolted. "When the masses are poor and hungry..." he had said, "...without land to grow their crops and yet there is land available, it is foolish to expect them not to take it. Hunger is a powerful motivator, it doesn't wait. When people are desperate, a deed written on a scrap of paper has little value."

She told him there was loneliness in her childhood, but that there were also many good memories. She told him of a time when she was fourteen. She had forgotten most of that day and what led her to the words she remembered, but the memory kept coming back to her and she could not rid herself of it---of sitting under the shade of a wide veranda with her best friend from childhood, talking of what they would do when they grew up. When her friend asked her what she would do, she answered, "I will follow what I feel in my heart." Then she added, "I will always reach for my dreams." The words were bright and alive, like springtime.

"But what are your dreams," her friend asked.

"I'm not sure."

"So, how will you find out?" But she had turned away from her friend, her eyes watching idly, without expression, a group of laborers cleaning dead limbs from a row of fruit trees. The question hung in the air, unanswered.

Abby Casal looked across the terrace and smiled. She could not remember the beginning or the end of that day, but she could still recall clearly and plainly, the words she had spoken twenty seven years ago. She did not know why they had remained with her or what significance had preserved them when so much else had been lost, nor why, remembering them again, she was filled with a prevailing feeling of hope. She had lived with the words, but they had given her no answer. Yet, there were occasional moments that came from the words, flashing moments of light, guiding lights, still strong, clearing the haze from her sight and showing her the way.

Far below the city twinkled in the darkness, stars hung in the sky, bright and quiet; and, suddenly, from

And The Mountains Cried

somewhere out of the soft blue air of that summer night, a coyote howled, and then there were more. Abby had heard them before, but never like this. It wasn't yipping or howling, it didn't sound like coyotes at all---a symphony of voices rising and falling across the mountains, weaving themselves into a curious harmony, mournful and full of longing and strangely sweet. Neither Matt nor Abby said anything, they only sat and listened, suspended in the serenity of the moment, balanced there, on a shaft of air, free of ties or claims, unburdened by responsibilities, by worry about the future or concerns of the past; and in that moment their worlds became as one.

The last ululations began to drift away, dying in gentle, careless rolls, until they were quiet. Abby drew her hand away, which she had unconsciously lain on Matt's. When she heard her own voice, it seemed to meet the last echoes of the singing. "Why does it sound so sad?" she whispered. Matt said he didn't know. "It was beautiful," she said, "but so sorrowful."

"We all have to make our peace with sorrow."

"I know," she said, "and with the feeling of being alone." And as she spoke the words, it seemed the mountains had closed in around her, grumbling in their vastness---the press and anguish of times past, when she had reached out in the empty silence to another heart for comfort, to talk with someone, to John, or to God; trying to negate her sadness and find peace with life.

Greg Gannaway

When her eyes moved to Matt's face, she saw a settling calmness, only the skin of his temples seemed pulled tighter and the planes of his cheeks drawn slightly inward, faintly more hollow than minutes before. It made his face look pure and young and she knew that of all those years behind her, this was her place, her moment, and the world for which she had been waiting.

As the night wound down, they talked of everyday things, past and present, laughed happily, feeling the rush of the evening, light and free---all restful, unencumbered, as if floating in the darkness, beyond the mountains, beyond gravity, hovering along the edge of the earth. She hoped he would not leave too soon.

"I'm glad I came, Abby."

She saw his eyes sparkle and smiled softly. "Are you hungry?" she asked. "We can eat whenever you like."

A sense of warmth permeated the kitchen where they dined. With only minimal persuasion, Matt had two helpings of everything. For dessert they each had a scoop of ice cream slipping about in the center of red bowls.

"I hope you like strawberry," Abby said.

"It's my favorite."

"Mine, too."

Outside a soft wind blew the trees in the cool mountain air.

And The Mountains Cried

C H A P T E R   1 0

Abby placed the dishes in the sink, turned to Matt and asked if he would like to have a glass of brandy on the terrace.

"Sounds good," he said.

She poured the brandy and picked up a glass with each hand. Matt walked across the room before her, opened the wide glass door and took a step back.

"Just leave it open, Matt," she said smiling as she passed under him..."let in some fresh air."

Matt waited as she placed the two glasses of brandy on the small iron stand and they sat down together.

The glow of the patio lights enclosed them within a barrier of darkness. She leaned forward, seeing only the darkness, but feeling the hint of some unknown promise laying beyond its barrier and suddenly she felt

Greg Gannaway

her life being stripped down to the simplicity of this one moment, a moment of joy too full to express. She turned to Matt and saw that he was not looking into the darkness. He was looking at her.

He had been sitting in his chair watching her, struggling, feeling things which he had forgotten he could feel, had never felt. Urges overwhelmed him: the touch of her hair, her body, the softness of her breast, and thoughts of a life shared. He turned away, yet she seemed more intensely real when he did not look at her. He took a deep breath, leaned his head back and looked into the great twinkling spread of sky, feeling their moments together weren't just moments, they were gifts.

He turned back to her and she smiled; it was a soft smile, but it was a smile of certainty and she knew in that instant that he was not a stranger, that he had never been a stranger. The thought was so brief she caught it just as he raised his glass to the level of his shoulders and said, "Here's to eyes that look into mine and hands I've never held. Here's to lips I've never kissed and maybe someday I will."

Abby seemed almost unsurprised by the words, as if she had wanted to hear them. She touched her glass to his and wanted to say, 'Kiss them now,' but she only nodded, feeling a sense of helplessness, the helplessness of finding a man for whom she had no right to seek.

And The Mountains Cried

They sat sipping brandy, their chairs turned slightly inward. She watched him empty his glass with a brief, single movement of his hand, a few drops spilling on the square of lace napkin that lay on the small iron table between them.

"More brandy?"

He glanced at his watch, "Bedtime for children under ten and architects. I need to be at the site early…I better go."

Abby did not stir or breathe for some seconds. Her body was warm, and yet an unaccountable shiver seemed to be running slowly along her spine. What had brought him to her, she wondered. Who was he, this man, arriving out of nowhere; a lost stranger…

In those few blank moments, there was only silence and the motionless outline of his face. She wondered what had been the purpose of their meeting---and what if she never saw him again? She wanted to shout: 'Don't leave, have more brandy, stay longer…' and wished tomorrow's sun would never rise and the night would last forever.

She wrapped her arms around herself as she walked with him through the garden. When they reached the wooden gate, he opened it and turned to her.

"Thanks again for dinner," he said, "it was great." Then he looked straight into her eyes, as if he had heard the cries she had not uttered. He wanted to put his arms around her and say, 'Come with me tonight, somewhere, anywhere, far away, it doesn't matter,' but sensing her confusion, he stopped himself. The expression on her face was one he had not seen. He saw her smiling, but it was a smile of sadness and the sudden change in her eyes made him certain that she knew what he was thinking. Then her eyes dropped and she waved her hand in an unconscious gesture. "No," she whispered, her voice falling away, "…I can't…it's too late…"

"Abby, I…?" He spoke her name, but could not continue, his voice faint, seemingly no more than the release of his own breath.

She glanced up at him, and he knew what he saw in his face. He stood oddly still for a long moment, then extended his hand and touched her arm lightly before turning and walking to his van. In one quick motion, he swung himself behind the wheel and started the engine.

There was only the faintest contraction of a smile on his face as he rolled down the window. "Bye, Abby," he said, "take care of yourself."

She saw his eyes remain on hers a moment longer than he had intended, then the van moved slowly down the twisting black ribbon of road, red tail-lights flashing through the trees. Raising her arm, she waved quietly, wishing she were out there with him as he disappeared into the silence.

The breeze had died and the leaves hung still as she made her way back through the garden into the house. The house seemed cold and empty. She stood inside

And The Mountains Cried

for only a moment, then opened the glass door onto
the terrace and walked across the tile floor until
stopped by the heavy stone railing. The night was
warm and clear, bright with stars. How quiet it
was…and still. Was it possible that all about her,
unheard by her ears, the air was filled with cries of
joy---and louder still, the cries of fear, that the stars
gazed down upon the mountains with love, and
promise, and despair---that they forgave her for what
she was feeling, forgave the world, forgave everyone?

She had always known the thing she wanted in life.
She had felt it here, on the terrace with him, a feeling
which seemed the meaning of spring, the first blue of a
gray sky. Her eyes looked down into the vast,
soundless motion of lights across the city and she
could feel the rise and fall of her breath, unable to stop
the thing that placed his figure before her---his figure
as she had seen him standing on the terrace. She could
feel nothing more, no wish, no hope, reducing her to a
mere sensation, draining her of energy, of
understanding, of judgment, of control, leaving her
without strength to resist. Then she heard it: a thin,
muffled sound of helplessness, creeping up through
her heart into her throat. She tried to turn back into
the house, but only slumped against the railing, unable
to react or move. And from somewhere within her,
not as a demand, but as some luminous point of
judgment, she could feel the presence of something
watching her, as if asking: Are you, at this moment,

damning your life, your vows to John, by your very
desire? She heard a moan muffled in her throat,
knowing that she did not have to hear the words, she
knew them, she had always known them. They were
words she did not want to hear and hoped that
someone would step from the shadows to help her, to
wipe the words from her mind. She tried to rise and
walk back into the house, but was incapable even of
that, and slumped further down, clasping the heavy
stone balusters. She sat still on the terrace floor, the
tiles were hard and cool under her body. She was past
the point of struggle; she remained there until late into
the night.

And The Mountains Cried

C H A P T E R   1 1

Matt awoke early, ate breakfast at the hotel restaurant and drove to the site. His office was now a rented construction trailer that Juan had arranged to have delivered to the site before he left Texas.

After squaring away his office, he turned his attention to the work at hand, studying the position of the sun and the long, early morning shadows stretching over the ground. He stood along the edge of the property for a long while, then walked down the slope to the crumbling ruins of Juan's childhood home.

There was always an electric feel to the start of a new project, a kind of nervous energy that seemed to jump things up inside. Already he could visualize the placement of the houses along the ridges; not as a structure where the houses were squeezed together by common walls and one was placed above another, but as individual cottages, each a small, private home, with intimate patios and views of the city of Monterrey in the distance.

His hand reached out, grasping the bristol board, and he began to draw; his pencil moving smooth and free, accenting a few sharp strokes along one edge and fading them out along another. He rocked the pencil, alternately back and forth and, at times, held the point full against the paper for clean, uniform strokes.

The lines formed houses of stucco and glass. He flung them across the board, there size and structure making successive steps in a series of terraced gardens. Then his hand slowed and he began to form the different levels. He would briefly stop, then continue in separate movements, stressing the vast views of the city.

Each house was efficiently sized, standing free of the other, a diverse mix springing from multiple thoughts, as none were of the same shape. Walkways curled through the ridges, there were stone steps, trees, a club house, tennis courts and a community swimming pool. By late afternoon the project lay before him, a three-dimensional reality, powerfully expressed in crisp, sparkling shades of darks and lights.

The houses seemed not to have been designed by Matt, but by the ridges and slopes on which they were to stand; each house a small mass, all flowing together in consummate harmony with the rise and fall of the land, as if natural elements of the terrain.

It was a simple concept and Matt knew the sketch was preliminary, but the design held a certain tension and he felt satisfaction with its simplicity.

During the next six weeks he worked feverishly to complete the plans. He did not think of Abby often, but when he did she came to him in sudden recollections, a persistent presence from the first day they met.

She had not come to the site and he was not sure if he expected her. Their evening together had been great and he had enjoyed the dinner…maybe that's where it should end. Still, the thought of her remained.

It was strange to think of her in such a way, as a close, pressing need, a need he could not qualify as either pleasant or painful. Yet, for reasons he could not grasp, it had become important to know that she existed in the world, that she was safe; it was important to think of her, of how she awoke each morning, what her days were like, did she sleep well. He wondered if any lingering thoughts of him had remained with her and, in those moments, felt the same wrench he had been fighting since first seeing her; the feeling of being unable to forget her face.

Abby awakened the next morning after only a few hours' sleep. She lay in bed, pressing her fists to her eyes. It was desire. It was that one single emotion that swept everything away, everything but the guilt under the desire; guilt for wanting a man she had only just met.

She pressed the curve of her palms into the quilted mattress and lifted herself from the bed, standing awkwardly for a moment before walking to the bathroom and switching on the light.

She let her bath water run warm, almost hot, brushed her teeth and stepped down into a sunken tub standing beneath a pool of light in the center of a polished granite floor. She laid in the water for a long while, feeling its warmth on her skin, her head leaning back against the rim of the bowl.

She did not want to think of Matt Callahan, but her mind had leaped to him the moment her eyes opened. In some unstated way, yesterday had been like an instantaneous discovery of life as she had always imagined. It seemed to come to her almost from the first moment she saw him.

That she had never felt this way about John, in all the years they had been married, made her close her eyes in sadness. It was something she had been unable to overcome; a shameful secret, not to be shared, made real because she wanted to feel fully the love a wife should have for her husband. She pressed her

And The Mountains Cried

fingers to the hollows of her temple and held them there---the thought only made her guilt worse.

She dressed quickly. Her dress, pale and simple, gave her the fragile appearance of innocence.

Because the sky was bright that morning, and she knew it would be clear and warm in the forest, because she wanted to see no one and knew she would be alone, she walked outside, across the covered veranda shading the back of her house, across the green lawn that Pedro had recently mowed, into the woods beyond, the soles of her white leather sandals leaving faint prints in the soft ground.

She walked slowly down narrow trails that seemed to have no end, her arms crossed over her breast, her hands clasping her shoulders, feeling huddled and intimate, knowing that if she were lying in Matt's arms, in the sight of all to see, her betrayal would be no less terrible; a violation created by a loneliness that seemed always to be with her. It was not the world she expected or wanted.

Once, on a spring day, when only fifteen, she remembered standing between two long rows of trees. She noticed how their trunks converged to a single point in the distance and began to feel the presence of someone beyond that point---no, not any of her friends---but someone whose presence she had always felt and whose world she had wanted to share. It was her love for that someone that had kept her moving forward, hoping to find him, and to be worthy of him

on the day when they would stand before each other
face to face. But since her marriage to John, she had
struggled to remove the presence of that someone
from her mind, her thoughts, wanting never to meet
him, hoping it was a name she would never learn. Now
she asked herself, 'Was it true what I was feeling on
that day?' She made a feeble gesture with her hands, as
if to push back the answer and wondered why she had
come here---hoping to wash it all away, hoping to
forget that person in the distance. But she knew why
she had come, because now that person had become
real and his name was Matt Callahan.

Through the leaves the sun shown yellow in the
shadowy air; she heard the soft sound of her own
footsteps on the grass; and above her the whisper of
the wind in the trees. The sounds seemed hushed and
far away, they seemed to come from another time,
from somewhere in the past, long ago. She walked on,
as through the quiet arches of a dream, feeling as if he
might appear in the next bend of the path and she
would hear him say in a gentle voice, 'We belong
together. Have we ever really been apart?'

She stood with the sun on her back, the light
becoming a bright edge around the darkness of her
hair. She closed her eyes, trying to escape the image;
but the image remained, and she knew she could no
longer deny her feeling, that she wanted him in the
most primitive way, here, now, in the open air, under
the long, waving, gray moss, without guilt, because it

would define that special sense of life she had never known, and because she had dreamed it long ago.

She did not know how far she had gone or what effect the distance had on her, but she walked on, pushing herself, the ground like an upward thrust against the strength of her legs. Now her legs were tiring, she felt heavy and eased herself down onto the grass. She rolled over on her back, not moving; the grass resisted, then gave way, conceding a faint outline of her body.

"Oh, God, no," she whispered, "this can't be happening."

She pressed her hands to the ground, feeling the weight of the sky like a heaviness against her body. High above, leaves hung motionless, only a scattered few were still green; the rest were brown, a light, crispy brown, hanging dead, awaiting the winter winds to scatter them across the earth.

She lay still in the grass for a long while, a swell of memories rummaging about in her mind; memories of times past, when she had imagined all the joys of life stretching before her---joys which she had never found; joys which she had come to know only in her dreams. They were dreams that didn't seem like dreams, even as she dreamt them, full of anticipation and complete, utter delight---the kind that faded away as the real world crept into her consciousness. And when she awoke there was sadness, knowing that such happiness was found only in her dreams, that her great sense of joy was always lost upon her return to reality.

She thought of that because, for the first time in her waking existence, she had suddenly felt those joys; felt them the instant her eyes fell on Matt Callahan's face. It was as if the past and present had smashed together in a single jolt, fusing all her hopes and passions into that one moment.

How long had it been? Had it been too long for all of this? She felt guilt's unwanted appearance rising within her; she wanted to shout: 'But don't you understand---I belong with him.' She closed her eyes, feeling the tug of those words, like an invisible string, tying her to them, knowing they had always been with her, and that since her marriage to John, she had lived in dread of their ever coming true.

She did not remember the walk back, of crossing the lawn and going into her house. At the top of the stairs she stopped, feeling almost unaware of her body's existence, as if she were moving away into some greater realm. She felt light, lifted, and it seemed to her that she had walked up the stairs without touching them, that the walk to her bedroom had been weightlessly easy. Her eyes moved about the room with abnormal clarity. She did not realize that she was looking through the eyes of a person from whom the concept of doubt had been removed, and what remained was the simplicity of a single decision; and that the thing which had been torn open before her

And The Mountains Cried

had not come from the sensation of joy and hope, but from the certainty of knowing what she must now do.

She felt the start of something cold forming inside her throat, it cut her breath for a moment and she shut her eyes tightly, trying to get herself back together. And in that anguishing moment, with the full, luminous understanding of everything that had happened, she knew that she could not stay. It seemed not a sudden decision, only the undercurrent of something she had felt from the moment Matt had driven away, an unconscious thought to free herself from the vows of her marriage to John.

Late that evening she got into her car and drove into the darkness, down the twisting mountain roads of Chipinque, a shimmering net of lights, delicate as lace, flashing through the trees from the city below. It seemed only the mountains could offer her some slim hope of relief and as she left them the ache in her heart only deepened.

C H A P T E R   1 2

How little we know what lies beyond our sight. We are taught that God created the universe and that it is endless and infinite. Never can we imagine it. Time, eternity, infinity are merely words to us, full of mystery and secrets. We do not comprehend them as we would that of a precisely drawn shape, or the flatness of a table. There is no image in our mind of infinity, we conceive of it only in terms of it being inconceivable. We hold our breath and look into the darkness between the stars, those holes in time into which the light of yesterday flees forever without a sound. How the heart longs to understand, and somewhere, at the farthest boundaries of our thoughts, there is the slight hope that this vast abyss, with its stars and planets, will condense before us and the mystery will be solved. Failing, we are left with only an empty silence that brings us about full circle and, in the end, we are back where we began.

Juan Sanchez believed in God, the Father, the Son and the Holy Ghost, and that if he carried his dream through to the end, it would be a victory, not just for him, but for those who suffer. But Juan was also a realist and believed his dream would not come true without hard work, persistence, a little luck, and help from the good lord above. "Beyond is beyond," he would say, "and only in death will mortal man find the answer."

Now, in the early morning hours, lying in the bed where he had slept for twenty years; under the roof where he had replaced the old cedar shakes with new tin, he tried to make sense of the thoughts rising and clamoring about his head, as if the purpose of his life had suddenly come to a halt. But he knew that was not true, that it was only a pause in time, and that the path of his future lay south to Mexico.

Little by little he drew himself up out of the daze of sleep, showered, dressed himself and, in the soft darkness of an early June morning, before daylight had struck its blow, and the ground still lay asleep under a spread of light dew, stepped through the screen door onto the deck of his cabin and started for his truck.

He stopped. Looking into the darkness, he could see the dim outline of Samson standing along the edge of the deck, still as a boulder. Juan took a couple of steps toward him and held out his hand, but on this morning Samson did not come to him. It was as if all the days and years they had spent together now stood, shoulder to shoulder, on the deck between them blocking his way. Juan waited silently for several moments, then dropped his arm to his side, stepped down off the deck and got into his pickup truck. As he pulled away he looked back and saw Samson still standing in the darkness, watching him go, as though, through some perception unique only to Samson, he knew he would never see Juan again.

Juan was leaving Texas with everything he owned, he left before dawn, so that when the land again became visible, there would be no sight of his home along the limestone banks of Bear Creek, no sight of the majestic live oaks, the blue-stem fields waving in the breeze; he would never again hear the slow pull of the windmill, or flights of duck sweeping low along Bear Creek, talking, their keen eyes seeing only time and far away things. All would be gone like a scrape in the wind, as if a whole life had been lived and ended.

Upon completion of the drawings, Matt had sent for Juan. Two days later Juan arrived at the site of his childhood home. He stepped out of his pickup truck, flexed his stiffened back, and stood facing west shading his eyes. When his vision cleared, he saw Matt sitting next to the doorway of the construction trailer, tilted back in a metal chair.

And The Mountains Cried

"I don't understand what took you so long?" he said jokingly.

Juan waived, then rounded the back of his truck under a row of elms and walked to where Matt was sitting. He smiled. "Champ," he said, nodding in a fatherly manner, "you don't want to let yourself get upset over things you don't understand. We're all a mystery to each other. I knew a girl once thought me hardly worth talking to, and no bigger than a grasshopper. But to that same grasshopper, jumping through the air, by the time I caught him and put him on a fish hook, I was a striding nightmare, big as a giant."

"Who was right?"

"Well, I don't figure either of them knew me for who I really was. I was a mystery to them." He paused for a moment, and then…"You know what a mystery is, Champ?" It's something you got no words for…something you just can't explain. That girl I knew never had the right words for me. The way she saw me, I was a grasshopper."

Matt smiled, glancing at him curiously, looked again. There was no weariness in his face from the long drive, only the reflection of an inner glow---the glow of delight and triumph. Had he, at that moment, possessed the ability to form his own image of Juan Sanchez, this was the vision he would have seen: the figure of a purposeful man determined to complete a lifelong dream.

"Champ, I always knew this day would come,"

There was an instant's pause, then Matt said calmly, "Well, it's here, you made it happen." His voice held the tone of congratulations.

That Matt had designed the project for his friend, who had pictured it long ago, had always known of it and had said, with growing confidence, that it would happen, removed any lingering doubts in his mind of the project being built.

They sat with their backs to the trailer, looking out over the site, grass flurrying beneath their feet from a breeze with little sound. Matt pointed out the general location of where the houses were to be built, explaining their relationship to the site and to each other. Then he rose from his chair and motioned for Juan to follow him down the slope, through the future rooms.

"Did you understand what I was saying?" he asked.

"Every word, Champ, houses should have honesty and dignity, just like people."

Juan spoke the words evenly, with meaning, and in that moment there came the hint of something rising before him, like the first thrust of a seed breaking through; earth and sky became still, windless, their colors pure and peaceful. And there in the stillness, in that motionless haze of air, he began to see the outline of small houses slowly forming along the hillsides; dimly at first, but it went on, a moment that seemed to make all things possible, as if he were caught in an

And The Mountains Cried

illusion of childish wonder. Yet everything seemed proper, the vision unrestrained, becoming clearer, growing, as if part of a known reality. He saw walls of stucco rising from the ridges; and windows---wide, clear windows, that opened the rooms to the brightness of the sun. His dream, he thought, the sense of it made real by the words Matt had spoken; like a common language between sight and sound.

He had always been able to name the thing he wanted in life. Now he saw it here, in its final setting, and from the words rose the vision of what he had always imagined.

After a long moment he glanced about him, remembering where he was and that he was not alone. Matt had been curiously watching him from only a few steps away. As Juan turned their eyes met in a glance of understanding. Juan smiled and knew the vision he had seen was as Matt had told him.

"Was what I just saw real, Champ?" For a moment it seemed almost as if Juan was not aware of his question. He was looking straight at Matt, but the focus of his eyes still retained the remnants of his vision.

Matt smiled. It was a silent greeting to a moment in which he was glad to be a part of. "It will be," he said, "it's up to you now."

They stood for a long moment, facing each other, as if at a formal gathering. Then Matt turned and Juan followed him up the slope into the construction office.

Matt took the drawings from a wide, flat metal file and spread them out on a layout table. His hand moved in a wide arc over the white sheets, pausing at times, pointing and explaining certain details. He did not speak of beauty, but of wall sections, elevations, structural components, cabinets, plumbing stacks, mechanical ducts. Juan leaned forward, his hands on the edge of the table, fingers stretched wide apart, feeling himself being carried forward on a wave of exultation, the little houses blooming before him. He saw their simplicity, their beauty, his eyes traveling over every line. Then, from beneath the heavy curve of his weathered brow, he lifted his eyes and looked at Matt, holding the glance purposely, quietly, his words expressed in the features of his face before they were spoken.

"Thanks, Champ, what you've done here is wonderful."

There was a faint suggestion of a smile on Matt's face, making the wink of his eye more intimate a thanks than words. Then he moved his hand to turn another sheet of the drawings, reading the one beneath, his hand moving in unconscious perfection, allowing each drawing to remain in view for long moments of time.

For hours, while Juan listened and the sky darkened and lights began to flair in the windows of the city below, Matt explained the design.

And The Mountains Cried

It was during the months of construction that followed, that Juan, in the clear, precise voice of a military report, would recalled the design of each house, explaining their method of construction to his men with the swift, clear-cut confidence that came from remembering every word Matt had spoken.

CHAPTER 13

Abby returned to Monterrey, and for weeks she
walked through the rooms of her townhome,
aimlessly, without purpose, as if to hasten each day
along, force time to pass more quickly. The evenings
were the worst. It was usually around dusk that she
would stop at the windows of her bedroom, look out
and see the dark outline of the mountains rising before
her; see the sun sink slowly behind their jagged shapes.
She had tried to avoid such moments; she had tried to
stop herself from going to the window. Her efforts
had failed; at the end of the day, drawn by some
unbending force, she would find herself standing
where she had stood the evening before, looking out
into a tearing stab of darkness.

And The Mountains Cried

Weeks passed in a jumble of disconnected days, each given to fighting the compulsion of a single desire, and the blinding struggle of bringing herself back into some form of normalcy.

Then one evening, while standing at the window in the darkness of her bedroom, something seemed to have momentarily veiled her sight, and she felt as if the mountains had vanished. For how long she remained at the window she did not know, only that she was startled by her own thought. Suddenly, sternly, she told herself that she had merely returned to Monterrey for no other reason than having simply wanted to; just that; nothing else; no other reason at all.

What had it been, anyway, she thought---just some will of the wind meeting, a night on the terrace, a summer thing---and this man, of whom she knew very little, who seemed to come out of nowhere…this wasn't his real life, this foreign country and these mountains…once the houses were designed, he'd go back to his own, to his work and his life in Texas.

Turning, she marshalled her strength and walked away from the window. It was her last chance to be free.

She walked swiftly, easily, in sudden relief. Yes, she thought…all she had to do now was focus on other things, forget his face, his name, and keep herself busy. Life would be simple.

She called on old friends, started an exercise routine, went to comedy movies, listened to music. She even tried painting to keep him at bay, but it was hopeless. Everything she did only drew him closer. She would hear him coming in the footsteps of John's nurses moving through the house or the continuous hum of the crowded streets below. She would feel a sinking gasp inside, that hidden feeling of guilt and desire which he always gave her. She didn't want to feel it, she tried to push it away, but it kept on coming, soft, shapeless, melting into her and she knew she had no power to stop it.

One evening an acquaintance of John's dropped by unannounced. He was a celebrated writer. He was pale and slender; he had wet, soft lips, and pleading eyes. Abby ushered him to John's room. As he looked into John's face, his voice slowly faded into silence, as he could see that what remained of John was only mental emptiness. After a brief visit it seemed time to leave. Abby had not noticed the attention with which he had watched her during his short stay. As she walked him down the hall to the front door, she felt him moving hesitantly closer, then he touched her arm and leaned his head to her ear. She heard his voice whispering things she had never expected. She jerked away from him and stood motionless for a moment, a sudden flash of anger in her eyes. Then she walked quickly to the door, flung it open and, as he crossed the threshold, slammed it behind him, hoping the crashing sound would wipe him from her memory, from existence.

And The Mountains Cried

She turned, shivering, and walked down the hall until she reached her bedroom. Such incidents had happened to her in the past; only then she hadn't been married, and it hadn't been by a close associate of her husband's.

She looked about her, at the soundless splendor of the room. She could see the outline of the mountains against the sky; tears welled in her eyes.

That night she dreamed of Matt, of their meeting in the restaurant; she dreamed it over again as it had happened. She saw him sitting next to the window, and heard him say as he had said then: "I was wondering if you could help me?" and how he had spread the map across the table. And in her dream she remembered the picture he had drawn for her.

She awoke the next morning with a sense of alarm, feeling that something wasn't right. She checked on John and then returned to her room. There were no sounds, only the suffocating emptiness of the house around her and she could feel the silence crashing against her ears. She pressed her fingers to the hollows of her temple. What was happening to her? Suddenly she wanted to get out of the house, into the open air, to run, to find relief. She hurried down the steps to the front door. When she reached the street she stopped, standing motionless, not conscious of the faces streaming past her; feeling only a strange detachment, alone with the distant clearness of his voice rolling through her mind. She recalled dimly his figure standing before her and she could feel nothing more, as if drained of all resistance, unable to think or understand, her mind reduced to that one desire, intense, it pulled at her, like hunger. She had to go to him.

That afternoon she raced toward Chipinque, her head lay back against the seat, her hands lightly holding the steering wheel. The sky was clear as a washed window, afternoon light flooded the road; it entered the car. She let herself relax in the bright illumination, feeling no bumping sensation, the wind and earth whistling passed, as if she were no more than an extended flash of motion suspended above the road.

When she reached the mountains she slowed her speed and leaned forward, holding herself high in the seat, feeling the grip of her hands tighten on the wheel. She had never liked driving on the narrow roads, but it was the first hint that she was nearing her home.

Pedro was first to see her black sports car approach the house, saw it slow to a stop at the top of the drive and watched as she got out of the car. She stood for a long while, just looking out across the lawn. The grass was a different green than she last remembered, mixed with tones of yellow. In Chipinque, yellow, it seemed to her, was the true color of fall, not brown, or blue; the fading grass, the clouds, the hazy sky, the leaves, all were now mixed with tones of yellow.

Light slanted through the trees, across the house, the lines of the roof blending into the misty, sunny air.

And The Mountains Cried

The wind had begun to blow from the north, across the mountains; it smelled clean, it brought the smell of winter. Abby wrapped her arms together, feeling the cool earth and sky closing about her. She loved this place, the fall, these mountains and everything that was part of it.

She saw Pedro as he approached and ask him to please move her car into the garage, then turned and waved to Josie, feeling the rough texture of the brick sidewalk beneath her sandals as she walked to meet her.

Upstairs Josie unpacked as Abby stood at the glass door of her bedroom looking out onto the terrace, fighting whatever it was that kept forcing thoughts of him into her mind. She had come this far, but still she did not want to think of his name, her mind holding to some dim form of defiance, half in defiance of him, half from the guilt she was feeling. And there was something else, the fear of him not wanting to see her again, that he might want to remove himself from her life, and that she would have to return to the emptiness from which she came.

Then one afternoon, standing in the living room of her mountain home, she realized that six days had passed since her arrival. She turned and, as if being pulled by a vacuum, opened the front door and stepped out into the garden, up the stone pathway to the heavy wooden gate. She was going to the site.

She was in no hurry and decided to walk the mile to the site, down Carrelera a Chipinque Road. She walked carefully, looking ahead into the late afternoon sun, seeing only the dark shapes of trees on either side of the road, their limbs moving faintly in the breeze.

As she walked it seemed as if there were other things, important things that needed her attention. They rose vaguely in her mind, but first, above all, there was the desire to see him, and the fear of never seeing him again, as if every step she took moved her further away from him instead of closer. Then she stopped, jerking abruptly. 'Is this what you want?' she thought, 'is it as simple as this?' and she knew it was not simple and wondered if she should turn back.

She stood somewhere along the edge of the road, alone in the silence of the mountains, fighting herself, fighting to move forward. She thought numbly, distantly: 'I mustn't go, it's too late...' She tried to turn and go back, but found herself walking forward. 'Don't,' she thought, but she did not stop.

She saw a van parked along the edge of the road and stopped again. She knew it was his van. She hoped it wasn't. She could see him tomorrow or not at all. She walked on until she stood by the van.

Then she saw him. It was his weightless way of standing that she noticed first. He was talking to a man holding a long metal rod. She saw him bend forward and point into a grove of trees, his face held in concentration. He straightened himself and continued speaking to the man, and they both laughed about something. Then he turned and began walking up the ridge.

He stopped under an arch of branches. She saw him looking through the trees at her. And though the air was light and clean in her mouth, it did not let her breath come easy. She felt the blood flowing through her veins and heard, in answering rhythm, the rush of the wind above her head, as the only sound filling the silence. She leaned against the van, bracing herself, knowing she could no longer stand without support. He stood for a long moment, his face raised to hers, disarmed and silent. Then, leaning forward, he started up the hill.

It all seemed so distantly familiar to her, almost as if it were a scene from one of her childhood dreams. He was coming toward her now, moving upward with long, smooth, rising steps. No, she thought, this was not a dream---it was real, as she would have seen it then, a moment's view of that person beyond the point whom she would one day meet.

As he got closer she began to distinguish the features of his face, the eyes and hair were as she remembered---the deep, perceptive blue eyes, the hair shaded in streaks of blonde that seemed to reflect the sunlight through the green of the underbrush; she saw a faint, half-smile on his face, his eyes looking at her as if it was all so natural that they should meet.

She was surprised that he moved toward her so quickly, that his hand gently held her arm, not as a greeting, but to give her support. He said: "Let's sit over here."

He led her across a green slope and sat her down on the steps of the construction trailer. She leaned back against the step above, feeling a flush of heat rise through her. He folded himself down beside her, his hand still holding her arm.

Then he moved his hand and, after a moment, she rediscovered her ability to speak.

"I thought I would drop by and see how the project was coming along."

"It's doing good....you walked here from your house?"

"Yes."

"Isn't that a long walk?"

"Not really."

They were talking like two people who had known each other for years and had never been apart. She didn't know why they had not greeted each other, couldn't say; only that it was like a continuation of something that had begun long ago.

Sitting motionless, she was inside herself now, floating, and the old life she knew seemed far away. She began to understand many things. She understood that this was only a moment out of a dream of time. She understood that as she drove her car up the twisting road toward her mountain home, toward a man she had only met, that it was right that she should now meet him here, and that something in her would find contentment in merely sitting by him, as she was at this moment, his face close to hers, and that she would want nothing more. And she understood that such contentment had been found by many people and that it was what she had looked for in John, the man she had married many years ago, the man with whom she had tried and failed to find love.

"Have you been here all day?"

"Since seven."

"I was still in bed then. Where did you have breakfast?"

"At the hotel restaurant...just coffee."

"At the same table where you and I met?"

"No, at the counter."

From the vantage of the steps on a high ridge they could see across the site, the little creek, the rise and fall of the ridges, the trees rising out of the fresh earth, pink ribbons fluttering from their trunks. She glanced at him and wondered of the hours he had sat alone thinking, drawing, and of all the wonderful designs that had come from those hours.

"Have you designed other projects like this?" she asked.

"A few…in Texas."

"Are these houses the smallest you've done?"

"I suppose, but that's not the way I think of it."

"How else would you think of it?"

"I don't think in terms of size. For me each house is a statement of someone's life, someone's dream, separate and distinct. I try to interpret that dream and bring it into physical reality. For the people who understand this, a house becomes a visible identity to their life, more personal even than their choice of clothing or furniture."

He was looking into a tangle of bare branches. He was as she remembered. There was that same sense of lightness in him, in his expressions, his mouth, his eyes.

"Matt…" Her voice was faint, but she had pronounced his name as if she wanted him to hear her say it, as if something had been done and settled between them long ago, and that it was inevitable that they should simply sit quietly together and talk.

He noticed her hand flat against the steps. He moved his hand and let it rest against hers. She felt comfort in his touch, letting her fingers hold his in answer to his closeness.

"Matt, do you mind if we just sit and talk…are you too busy?"

"Not for you."

She turned to him, smiling, and asked, "Who was that man you were talking to?"

"He's part of the survey crew. They locate where the houses are to be constructed and what trees are to be saved. The ribbon lets the contractor know which ones not to remove."

And The Mountains Cried

"Have you finished the design?"

"There might be a change or two, but it's pretty much done."

"Can I see?"

"Sure, it's an earlier perspective, but yeah...I'd like to show it to you."

He rose to his feet and nodded at the construction trailer. "It's just inside," the tone of his voice giving clear evidence that he was glad she was there.

He walked inside the trailer and returned with the sketch beneath his arm and motioned for her to follow him. "I want you to see it from where it was drawn."

Abby saw him walking before her; saw the grace of his movements, as if his body was a source of power that spread to everything around him, a power that kept drawing her ever closer to him.

They stopped at a point along the ridge. He turned to her and smiled, thinking her to be even lovelier than he remembered. As he folded the cover sheet back from the drawing, she found herself brushing lightly against his shoulder. He looked at her, neither hiding his feelings nor suggesting anything further.

"This is it," he said.

It was not the houses, not the pool, not the walkways or trees, but the layered tones, the crisp, black lines from which they were formed, that first caught her eye. The meaning of the day seemed held within the drawing. How could something so beautiful have been created with such a simple tool?

She thought of his fingertips pressed against the pencil, his long fingers continuing their straight lines through the sinews of his wrists, to the muscles of his arm, as he moved the pencil over the paper. She thought of this as she looked at the rendering, saw its power, it frightened her, yet she felt happy and strangely excited.

"It's beautiful," she said softly.

There was a simple confession of intimacy in the sound of her voice, more revealing than the words she spoke, but she spoke as if that was her wish. She asked many questions, her eyes moving from the site to the drawing. Matt explained the simplicity of the design: each house being inevitably what it had to be, that one had to follow the sweep of the land to understand the reason for their placement, a final expression of the ridges on which they were to stand; and that few trees would be removed, and would flow---like the spread of water---around and through the gardens.

There was a moment of silence, a sense of anticipation rose through her body, slowly, like warm mist, and she felt no desire to move or think, wanting only to hold to the moment and stand beside him on the grassy ridge in the late afternoon light.

"Abby," he said quietly, without hesitation, feeling the certainty of her answer would cause no stress. "You're going to have dinner with me tonight, aren't you?"

And The Mountains Cried

She turned away, as if struggling with some force outside of herself. The struggle, or the uncertainty---or whatever it was didn't last very long and when she turned back and faced him, he saw her lips move to form but one word.

"Yes," she said quietly.

At that moment she did not want to doubt her answer, for doubt would have been an admission of uncertainty. But she knew when she said 'yes' that she had waited for this and that it might break into pieces should she allow herself to be too happy.

CHAPTER 14

Abby entered the restaurant that evening and the warm, sweet smell of fall came in with her. She stopped just inside the doorway. She wore a white dress that fell from her breasts to her feet in soft folds of venetian silk, the luster of the cloth sensitively obedient to the movements of her body, as if wrapped in a sheet of radiance.

Matt stood along the edge of the entry, not quite believing what he saw. It was only after what seemed an endless span of time, that he was able to move forward, closing the short space between them.

"Abby..." he said, but his lips were unable to move beyond the effort of the greeting. After a moment's pause, he said: "Abby, I've missed you."

The words rose through her like warm liquid. She smiled softly, "I know...I've missed you too, and it's only been a few hours. Have you been waiting long?"

And The Mountains Cried

She could not name the nature of the glance with which he looked at her, but his face was strangely calm, as if coming to the end of a long search.

"All my life."

She felt the touch of his fingers holding hers. She had not remembered him taking her hand, it seemed so natural and what she had wanted since the moment of seeing him.

They knew they should turn and go to their table, but they did not turn and remained standing. She looked up at his face, as if in the moment of a magical dream, his smile telling her there was no place else to go and, in the high, vast air of the Sierra Madre Mountains, Abby Casal and Matt Callahan felt the world go still.

A crowd had gathered at the El Mirado restaurant, scattered in tables around an expanse of space reserved for dancing. The guests sat about in wide-eyed admiration of the surroundings, their voices ringing gaily against the concrete terrace. Candles stood trembling against the night sky; darkness made the flames seem brighter.

"This way please," said the hostess, smiling as she led them to their table. Abby felt the smoothness of a luxurious cloth beneath her hand, the leather of a curved chair behind her shoulders. The moon was full, like a haze of light hanging in space. They looked down on the city, at each other, silently, gently, as if the most beautiful words were those that went unspoken, and she saw in his eyes that he felt as she did, as if some compelling sense of understanding had formed between them.

She turned and looked across the terrace, its polished surface was like a pool reflecting the glow of the sky. She bent her head and rubbed her cheek against his hand, feeling light, free, lost in some other time, some other where or when…drifting, as if her body had no need for support and the chair on which she sat was merely a superfluous touch of elegance.

The waiter brought a bucket of ice with the champagne. There was the pop of the cork and the tinkling sound of the pale, gold liquid being poured into two glasses, bubbles rising through two crystal stems. Abby sat looking down into the bubbles, holding the stem of her glass between two slender fingers. Weaving reflections of candle light played on the golden liquid, her eyes, and from somewhere in the distance and yet not far away, a song could be heard.

It was a song written by an old Spanish composer. He was not known by many, but Abby had discovered him and she loved his music.

> Night Don't Go Away
>
> Let it be forever
>
> But should the end come soon
>
> Take me for what I am
>
> And do not ask of tomorrow

And The Mountains Cried

"Oh, Matt," she breathed, "I can't tell you how I've dreamed of an evening just such as this…I know that's sentimental, but I suppose I am…I love being here with you on such a beautiful night."

After a moment, she put her head on his shoulder, eyes closed, listening, flowing in and out of the hidden promises held within the words of the song. For just one night she thought, while it lasts, it's all right to let yourself dream, to forget everything and just feel. When had she ever felt it before?

He felt her move closer and squeeze his arm.

"What are you thinking, Abby," he asked.

Her answer was slow and gentle. "I'm thinking how beautiful the world is; that it was beautiful yesterday and a thousand years ago and how it will still be beautiful tomorrow…no matter what happens."

"Tomorrow…" he said, "…how can we know…?"

"But, Matt, we do know…tomorrow is always…"

"Always is a big word," he said. "it's like forever."

"Forever is tomorrow, it's tomorrow and tomorrow…it's always there, waiting for us…"

It seemed to Matt that her eyes grew clouded as she lifted them, soft and trusting, to his, and he knew that she was begging him to believe her, and that he had to believe her because if he didn't, there wouldn't ever be anything else for them.

She saw him looking at her. It was a glance with which he had looked at her on her patio and she wondered of the meaning of what she now felt. She closed her eyes, not wanting to think of it, and then she knew she did not have to think. The words were simple and right, and she could feel the closeness of his presence, as if the orchestration of life as she had always dreamed.

"The name of the song is Night Don't Go Away," she said. "It's about two people from different worlds...like you and me."

She wore a touch of pale pink lipstick, her night-dark hair falling to the curve of her naked shoulders. Matt sat quietly, watching her. She could feel his eyes on her and found pleasure in his awareness. She had never felt more feminine.

"What are you looking at," she asked softly.

He smiled, "Only you...do you mind."

The clarity of his eyes seemed to have fused with the pale of the moon, a limitless depth into which she had now fallen. She reached out to him, letting her hand touch his cheek, feeling the settling warmth of his skin.

"I will always want you to look at me, Matt."

His eyes remained on hers, still, searching, stirred by hope, by the clear night, and something which he could not name.

They took in the evening, the dark, velvet shadows, sipping champagne, laughing, talking; the moon high in the black sky, its pale, gold color whitened like a wash of salt around its edges.

And The Mountains Cried

"You know," he said, "I can remember when I was a kid working construction…I thought of having an evening like this. I didn't think of it very often, only once in a while, when the moon was shining like tonight and I was tired and wanted nothing more than to lie down and fall asleep right where I stood. I thought that one day I would sit in a place like this, where a drink would cost more than what I made working all day, and that I would deserve every minute of it, every swallow of champagne, every flicker of every candle on the table, and that I would sit there for no reason other than my own enjoyment."

As he spoke, Abby began to sense a faint change in the expression of his face, as if recalling his youth brought back old pains, but he went on, his voice soft and steady.

"After I acquired a little money and saw what it could buy, I was surprised; it seemed the place I had imagined was not to be found. But I kept looking, until finally I came to believe that such a place did not exist. I gave up trying to find it long ago."

He lifted his arm from the table and closed his hand over hers, his eyes looking into hers.

"But tonight, here, with you, I've found it."

She made a helpless little gesture, as if to reach out to him, and he saw the beginning of a hidden sadness in her eyes.

"Oh, Matt, I…I'd give it all away, everything I've ever had in my life if we'd met sooner. I'm not used to

being happy, and now I'm happy and unhappy too."
And she added sorrowfully. "I've never felt this way
before."

He felt her hand trembling beneath his, then saw
her head bending down, letting her lips press softly
against the top of his hand; it hid her face in the
moment when her eyes filled with tears. When she
finally raised her eyes to his, he could sense her
unspoken emotion.

"Matt," she said, her voice strangely soft and sad,
"I'm going to miss nights like this…and I'll miss you,
truly I will."

He looked at her for a long while, not moving.

She drew a deep breath and started to say
something, then paused for a moment, as if trying to
reassemble her thoughts or decide whether to speak at
all.

"Maybe I've got things all wrong, but…" She
hesitated.

Matt leaned forward, feeling a growing tightness in
his throat.

There are moments in a man's life when the single,
steady beat of living changes. He suspected this to be
one of them.

"What do you mean, Abby…wrong about what?"

"What I'm trying to say is…is that I wished…Oh,
God, I'm making a mess of this…"

Matt settled himself and placed one of her hands in
his. "C'mon, Abby…"

She looked down, feeling a sinking gasp inside.

"…tell me what it is you want to say, whatever it is."

Her glance held to the smooth skin of his hands holding hers; she could distinguish single threads of hair on his arm. Then she raised her eyes to his. "I feel so mixed up, things are happening too fast…maybe I'm misunderstanding everything, but isn't there something going on between us…more than just the ease of being together?" She placed her hand over his, her lips closed softly, the shape of tenderness and wondering, "…isn't there…?"

Matt moved his hand over her forehead, along the line of her dark hair, feeling an emptiness for all the past years they had not been together.

"I knew it before you did," he said, "I knew it the moment you walked through the door of El Mirado."

She closed her eyes, letting the moment linger. When she spoke again there was a faint coating of certainty spread evenly over the soft notes of her voice; that things could not have been otherwise, that they were as they had, and ought to be.

"Thank you," she said.

"For what?"

"For making me feel as I do."

"How do you feel?"

Abby sat quietly for a moment, staring out into the night, feeling the struggles and worries of her past dropping away; and knowing that what she wanted most, at this moment, was to sit in this place, under the night sky, breathing in the mountain-sweet air and simply look at him. She smiled and said softly, "I feel happy, how could it be any more than this."

"I know," he said, "I keep thinking the same thing, just a summer night, but so nice."

"Yes," she said, "I only hope it's real."

"Tonight is real, Abby...we made it so."

She turned away with a slight gesture of despair. "But do we really know each other?" she asked.

Matt told her that it didn't matter. "I only know how it is for me," he said, "when I'm with you." Then he smiled, "What would you say if I ask you to dance."

The sparkle in her eyes held a hint of surprise. "Why, Matt," she said, turning to him, "I thought you'd never ask."

He watched as she walked onto the dance floor, the lights and shadows, the shifting movements of her dress. She glanced back once, turned and held her hand out to him. He did not realize that he had stood still in that moment and felt a slight shudder at regaining his awareness. It was then that he walked toward her.

They stood before each other, his tall figure, in colors of black and gray, stressed the long, firm lines of his body, relaxed, standing without effort. She let her head fall back and looked at him for only a moment, then dropped softly against him the length of her body, feeling his chest against her breast, the length of her legs pressed gently against the length of his, weightless, held upright only by the strength of his arm around her waist. The lightness of her wrist told her that her strength was now part of his and that she could move only as he commanded.

Ever so slowly they began to turn and sway, the light silk of her evening gown blowing in the soft breeze against his tall figure, the essence and form of unobstructed rhythm, there---and not there, moving as one body, one mind, feeling only the simple pleasure of being together. When the song ended, he did not let her go, but held her, as if the song were still playing; as if her closeness solved all problems, answered all questions.

She lifted her head. He saw her long lashes gently touching her cheeks and for a moment her eyes were closed; then she looked up at him and he placed both his arms around her waist, feeling through his fingers the effort of her body to let him hold her closer and he heard her whisper:

"The night is so beautiful, Matt...I wish it would last forever. It makes me think back to a time when I still believed all my dreams could come true. It's been a long time since I felt that way."

Another song streamed across the terrace, spreading through the night air, over the lights of the city below. It seemed to embody her every move and thought, and she began to feel a different sense of herself, as if dancing on the roof of the world. She brought her hand in close, resting it against his chest, feeling her cheek against his. He moved his arm farther around her waist and pulled her closer. Their movements were effortless, light, lifted, as if drifting with the wind and she thought that nothing within the whole of her life had felt so right.

The end of the song fell away into the darkness and Abby pressed herself close to him, murmuring his name, almost involuntarily, as if the sound of her voice came not from her lips, but from some element gathered out of the night air. For a moment she was afraid to open her eyes, for fear that she was in the midst of just another childhood dream and the reality of the moment would disappear. But when she looked, she saw in his eyes what she had felt when saying his name and she could feel herself there, standing in the moonlight, sensing the warmth of his closeness. She felt, distantly, that she should feel shame for what she was feeling, but it seemed as if any feelings of misgiving were not within her, but held by someone she had, at the moment, left behind.

Yet something did remain; flickering, running back and forth through her veins. She stood looking at him for a long moment. Matt had a feeling that suddenly she hadn't wanted any of this to happen, that she dreaded what was to come and wanted to ask him to please forgive her for what had happened, because she had no right to feel as she did.

And The Mountains Cried

He stood without moving, his face held no expression, but his eyes looked at her as if he were hearing the words she had not pronounced.

"Abby," he whispered, half as a question, half in reassurance, then he put his arms around her and kissed her, and it was like moonlight and honey. He could feel her shiver and told her there was no reason to be sorry, that there was nothing to forgive. She felt his hands move down the line of her bare arms and heard her own heart beating in the stillness.

Another song began to play, but the moment held them motionless, alone on the dance floor.

Matt backed away. He did not kiss her again, but took her hands and pressed them to his lips, not as a kiss, but as a gesture to wipe away the silence of all their years apart. She felt a shudder run through her body. When he lifted his eyes to hers, she tried to speak, but was unable to do so and realized that she was crying.

"Abby?"

She wavered for only a moment, searching his face, tears running down her cheeks, tears of joy, of happiness, as a woman in surrender to a love that, until now, she had never found.

He placed his arm around her waist, so that they moved only by his strength. He led her from the dance floor to the far edge of the terrace, where they sat on the edge of a low stone wall, her face buried in his shoulder like a lost child; the beauty of the night falling around them.

He did not try to stop her, he let her cry, cradling her, stroking her hair, his arm tight about her. She felt the security of his arm, a security which seemed to tell her that as her tears were for both of them, so was the security of his arm, as if giving her the right to break down, here, on this night, by telling her that he would carry what she could carry no longer---that, from this moment on, he would be there for her.

When she finally raised her head, she saw a faint movement in his face; it was not quite a smile, but it gave her the answer she needed, and she knew then that the story between them was somehow yet to be finished.

"Matt..." she whispered, her voice jerking unevenly, "I..." But before she could continue, he shushed her softly with only the slightest movement of his head.

"Don't talk, Abby."

She felt the power of his arm as he drew her closer and laid her head against his shoulder. It seemed to Abby that, through all the years of her waiting, she had found home; that somehow she had always known the feel and warmth of him. She wished the night would last forever. She wished they would last forever.

He ran his hand over her forehead, brushing the hair from her eyes.

And The Mountains Cried

"Don't say anything now," he said quietly. "We both know what it is that we must face, and we'll speak of it, but not now; now we can believe what we want to believe."

Then he smiled and patted her arm. The curve of his hand was warm and gentle and so were his eyes.

"Lot of stars out tonight." he said.

She snuggled closer to him and put her hand in his. "Whenever I look into the sky, it makes me think of all the places I'd like to go…I bet you've been everywhere, and done everything in the whole world."

Matt's eyes widened slightly as he inched his head back and smiled. "Well," he said, "I wouldn't say everything."

"Sometimes, I think that's what I want to do…see it all, do everything. But then there's times I don't feel that way at all. It's the same me, but still…"

She stopped, a star shot across the sky in a shimmer of arcing light and disappeared. She squeezed his hand, made a silent wish and burrowed deeper into his side.

"What places did you like best?"

"I like it right here in the mountains with you."

"I hope you mean it."

"Do you remember the little ridge we stood on this afternoon? I'd like to build a house right there, so I'd always be near you."

"I wish you would."

Greg Gannaway

Suddenly, out of the clear night, a swift-moving cloud swooped across the sky. Matt wrapped his hand around her bare shoulder, and when the fleeting shadows touched her, he felt a ripple of chill run up and down her arm.

"Are you cold?"

"A little."

"Think we ought to go?"

"Maybe."

"Do you want to?"

"No…but maybe we should. The weather changes in a hurry up here." She slipped her arm through his, and pulled him close. "Don't worry," she said smiling, "I'll look after you."

Abby didn't notice the faces of the people sitting at the different tables, some tapping the shoulder of their companions, glancing quickly as they passed, glancing away again. Matt let his hand trail behind him, fingers over her wrist, a slight pressure, like a touch of assurance, leading her along an edge of dim light that spread over the dance floor. She let herself be carried along without question, feeling her heart open to the world, to him, knowing that on this night they would be together.

And The Mountains Cried

CHAPTER   1 5

Matt's cottage was the first of four, a small, freestanding structure anchored into an expanse of weathered stone in the midst of a stand of timber; a spacious deck flung itself out into their gnarled branches.

The walkway shrank into a set of pale brick steps that led them to the foot of the door. After a few minutes, a few turns and several steps up, they stood before the entry, the light above the door spilling yellow across the stone landing. Abby watched as Matt placed the key into the lock and the door swung inward into the darkness. At the moment when the lights went on, Matt pulled the door shut, the sound of the lock clicking closed behind them.

Greg Gannaway

The cabin smelled clean and fresh. Abby moved about the room, noticing every object. It looked like the secret retreat of two people cut off from all ties to human existence. Her consciousness yielded to the sight of a beautiful rock wall. She turned to Matt and smiled faintly, feeling a slight nervousness.

She noticed a collection of candles on each of the end tables. Matt smiled and watched, tracking her passage from candle to candle, as she struck a match and held it to each wick until they all burned steadily. Across the room he opened the thinly laced curtains hanging over a line of windows on either side of two glass doors. He swung the doors open and looked up through the branches of the trees, stunned by the limitless stars and huge, bright face of the moon, its light falling across the deck and into the cabin, an endless field of dazzling silence. The sky had once again become clear.

He turned and switched off the lamp lights. The room was filled with the quietness of the night. They stood silently before each other in the flickering light. Then he moved slowly toward her and let his hands rest on her shoulders. She did not move, waiting, her heart pounding, looking at him with an unmoving glance. He kissed her softly, feeling the faint touch of her fingertips brushing his cheek, his neck. He drew her to him and gently turned her around and loosened the zipper of her dress. There was the rustle of delicate silk as it dropped to the floor. She wore no bra; the thin necklace glistened in the candle light. She let her glance follow the movement of her panties, as he slid them down the length of her legs. Then she stepped out of two silver triangle shoes and he began to slowly move his hands over her breast, circling the nipple gently.

"Oh, Matt, I…" Her voice faded and she swayed against him, tilting her head back with a slight moan, her eyes closed. He let his hands run over her body, his fingers crept down her belly, to her thigh and her body began to quiver. She turned to him and, in a gentle motion, helped him out his clothes and led him onto the bed. He felt her hand move over his bare chest, his stomach, touching, caressing, reaching down; he felt her fingers slowly stroking his rigid flesh. His hand moved down her thigh; he kissed her lips, her ears, her neck, felt her trembling as she moved one hand to his back and pulled him gently on top of her. For a moment he held himself above her, moving his chest slowly across her breasts. Then he was inside her, whispering words into her ear, kissing her, pulling her into him.

She cried his name out breathlessly, pressing her face into the curve of his neck, her body quivering. She arched and strained for more, wailing softly, moaning, crying out in incoherent phrases that had no ending, her skin against his, rolling beneath him, as if held in a coil of wind. Then she shook violently.

The end came in soft screams of ecstasy, as warm gushes of silky wetness drained from their bodies and they lay still and helpless. She felt the weight of his body on hers, panting and exhausted. She touched his cheek with her finger tips and nibbled his face, tasting him with her lips. He removed himself from her and let his head sink heavily into a white pillow. Then he turned her face to his and kissed her. Her lips parted invitingly, soft and warm, and he knew that what he felt for her would never come again in his life time. It seemed the ending of a great journey, light years of travel, always moving toward her, across the galaxies of time, to the warm, burning fires of this moment.

They lay together that night, falling asleep in each other's arms. They woke again, and slept, and woke, and watched the dawn come up over the mountains and spread itself across the sky. They breathed in the cool, fresh mountain air; it was a new day, a golden day.

Before they were dressed, Matt rose and closed the curtains, the morning sun filtering through the fine lace. She watched him as he turned and walked toward her and sat on the edge of the bed.

In a quiet tone he asked, "Abby, I would like to make a sketch of you…just as you are this morning; something only for you and me."

She smiled, then leaned up and kissed him.

"Yes, I would like that…I don't look very pretty, though."

And The Mountains Cried

Matt thought that if anything, she looked prettier than ever. Sleep seemed to have rested her eyes and left them dark and dreamy.

He pulled the small breakfast table to the middle of the room, making a stand for his drawing pad. It took a while to adjust the light as he wanted, and to place the table at the right angle. All the while Abby lay quietly on the bed, her head propped on a pillow, watching him. Once satisfied, he turned to look at her and, for a long moment, fell into a dazed silence.

"Is this what you want, Matt?" she asked.

He saw her body lying before him across the bed, only a small corner of the sheet covered her rounded hips. She seemed perfection itself, her dark hair tossed about her face, small-waisted, with creamy porcelain arms and shoulders, long straight legs, a delicate face…like some painting or statue of long ago, from the Renaissance, from ancient Greece. Her nipples were erect in the filtered light, lips parted; long lashes fell against blushed cheeks.

"God, Abby, hold it…like that."

He turned back to the pad on the table, feeling swept beyond accounting, as if not quite able to believe what he saw before him.

She posed in silence, and the room grew misty and unreal, filled with strange excitement. She watched his hands; saw them remembering her figure, building her form, drawing through lines, beginning again, slowly, patiently. She felt his power and suddenly it seemed there was no space between them and that his hands were moving, not over the drawing on the paper, but over her naked body and she closed her eyes, weak with a feeling of physical pleasure, wanting more of him, always more.

'Oh, God,' she thought, 'where do we go now?'

C H A P T E R   1 6

Through the next week they spent all their time together, talking of nothing in particular, content merely to be together, saying the small things that people say when they're happy, their feelings for each other held in the warm sound of their voices. She rode with him to the site, where they sat close in a little hollow of soft grass, under a gathering of oaks, looking down through the trees at the bright green of the rolling ridges, darker where the shadows fell, or where the wind passed. He talked of the houses, his arm outstretched into the warm air; palm down, sweeping along the lines of the terrain, as if lifting the houses from the soil, an instinctive completion of the words he spoke.

Greg Gannaway

Then she said, her voice low, quiet, unsteady. "Matt, I had a baby once…almost. It was a miscarriage, she was born dead. I wasn't married at the time. I don't know why, but I wanted you to know."

Something had made her confess it to this man from Texas. She had never told anybody, not even John, who she knew couldn't have handled it. She looked at him, not quite certain of his reaction. Matt smiled softly, gave her a blue-eyed look that she had come to love and placed his hand on her forehead like a word of comfort.

"It's okay, Abby."

In an instant she felt her heart tingle, timidly, trustfully, as if the touch of his hand gave her protection from all things.

"Put your arms around me, Matt. Hold me, like that."

She sat huddled against him, her cheek buried against his chest, legs curled beneath her, not moving, not ever wanting to move.

She whispered, "Thank you, Matt."

There was an evening when they were together in her living room. She was sitting on the couch, as she had done the first time they were together. He was leaning lightly against a glass door, hands in his pocket, gazing down into the thin, trembling lights of the city below. He would turn, look at her and smile. The smile said everything she wanted to hear. There seemed no need for words, as if the meaning of the moment was

held in the stillness of his body, a body for which
motion seemed as effortless as the ease of not moving.
And she wanted him not to move, to keep space
between them, because she wanted to watch him, to
feel the pure, simple eloquence of his being, his power,
as the final form of the dream that had kept her
moving; this man who would, perhaps, be the dream
she had so wanted to reach. She could feel her breath
gathering under her ribs, it pressed against her heart,
crept up into her head, her eyes. She saw herself and
him, all at once, as if their time together was a little
season of its own.

Outside moonlight spread a wash of silver across
the lawn, and she caught herself thinking that this was
the way she had always dreamed it to be and felt
suddenly certain that all was well, and that all the pain
and suffering in the world had, at this moment,
vanished.

After a long while, she walked to him, took his
hand in both of hers and held it against her cheek. It
seemed, at that moment, that whatever fears and
doubts she'd had melted away. "It's been a long time,
darling. I was afraid I would never find you." She said
the words simply, naturally, intimately, filling the
distance between them, as if her only reason for
breathing was to be with him.

There were nights when they would go upstairs to
the intimate surroundings of her bedroom, fling open
the doors to the terrace and, for many hours, talk

about their lives, their fears, their dreams. When they grew hungry, Abby would ventured down to the kitchen, make finger sandwiches, open a bottle of wine and return before Matt could even miss her.

The mountain air was cool and Matt would lay stretched out across the bed, his head propped in one hand. Abby sat with her knees under her chin, her back resting against the padded head board, content with her thoughts and being alone with Matt. And, as if swept away by the mountain breeze itself, she could feel her earlier twinges of guilt began to dissipate, and for the first time in years she felt almost free.

Little by little she told him about her father and how he had spent so little time with her when she was young. She told him about meeting John and how he had seemed so mature and dedicated, but, that after a time, she had become watchful of herself, conscious of trying to be the kind of woman she thought he expected her to be, and to feel for him as he felt for her.

"Did you ever want children?" he asked.

She raised her head and looked at him and he wished he hadn't asked. Abby did not answer immediately, taking a sip of wine, collecting herself. "We tried," she said, "but I always lost them. In the end it seemed to form a wedge between us."
She shook her head. "It's not that I don't care about him…I do, but what I feel comes from appreciation or duty or something…I don't know." She stopped and

pressed her fingers against her forehead, the thought awakening traces of the past. "I hoped I could change, that after a time, maybe I would come to love him as he loved me. But it never happened and, as the years went by, he came to see it too. It hurt him, I knew it hurt him, but the more he tried to bring us together the more suffocated I felt." She shook her head. "I know it makes me sound like a terrible person, but I can't help it."

"You're not terrible," Matt said gently. "You're only being truthful."

Abby sat quietly, staring absently out into the darkness beyond the terrace. "Several years ago John began to forget things, little things at first, later he couldn't remember how to get home from the office or even how to open a car door. So we visited a couple of specialist, and each of them told us that John was in the beginning stages of Alzheimer." She swallowed hard. "After that it just started getting worse. He faced it as best he could. Even up until he was barely able to walk, he still managed a smile from time to time. And every time I saw that smile, I could only think of the unfairness of it all, knowing that all he really wanted was for me to love him as much as he loved me."

She was quiet then, her face reflecting the turmoil of the past years. "I sometimes even wonder if I'm not partly to blame for John being sick…I mean because of the all the pain and anguish he's endured since our marriage."

Greg Gannaway

"Don't do that, Abby," he said. "It's not your fault, you can't take the blame for your husband's illness."

She did not speak or move, only nodded silently, her dark hair settling about her shoulders. They were silent for a long time. She noticed the soft light around them, the sparkle of the ice in her glass, then, in a low tone, she heard herself ask the question held within her like some secret torture, the question that had come to her again and again over the past few days. "Did we meet too late, Matt?"

Once only did he turn to look away, then reached across the bed and took her hand. It was a question which he had not expected and could never imagine as being true, not now, not ever. She waited for his answer, the silence settling heavily between them, but the question went unanswered and she did not ask again.

Turning his hand, she pressed her fingertips against the outline of his ring. She held them there, feeling relief from the hard, contrasting bite of the metal.

"What kind of ring is that?"

"It's my college ring."

"I've never seen one like it. It's pretty."

She didn't look up and through the dark curve of shadow covering her face, he saw a tear rolling down her cheek.

"Abby, what's the matter?"

Still she didn't look at him and he could but guess the sadness of her expression.

And The Mountains Cried

"It's going to be okay, Abby, really…we'll be fine."

"I know, that's just it, we're already so fine it makes my head spin. I've never felt this way before."

She raised her face and looked at him, trying to smile, wiping away the tears. Her eyes held the depth of the sky and in them he could feel the confirming warmth of a love he had never, until now, imagined. He moved his hand along the softness of her cheek, searching her face, thinking suddenly how delicately childlike and innocent she seemed at times, then raised the hand he yet held and pressed it to his lips, as if to answer the question for which he had no words.

Beyond the terrace, the earth rolled silent under the sky. Her eyes never left him, as if the night might steal him away if she looked aside for even a moment. She heard him speak of simple things: the wind and its cause, of wild geese coming high across a yellow moon, throwing their calls into the sky, their long necks thrust into the clear air.

"I've never understood how anyone could kill such beautiful birds," he said. And as he spoke the words, Abby saw the muscles of his face move briefly. He seemed bewildered, as if he knew full well that the killing would never end and that there was nothing he could do to stop it.

She sat silently still, listening, attuned to every word, hearing the chilled, lost tone of his voice. He spoke of these things as if trying not to move beyond the moment, to live within their time together.

Greg Gannaway

When she asked about his home in Texas, Matt was
hesitant for a moment and looked out through the
open glass doors into the night. "I wish you could see
it, Abby," he said. "I was foolish to have lived so long
in the city."

Then, with the clearness of a light peering into his
memory, he began to speak. "One day, as I was
jogging through the woods, it started to rain. It was
one of those days we get in Texas during the spring,
blue-gray clouds covering the sky. I love to run in the
rain, so I struck out in an easy stride, taking in the
weather with deep breaths, feeling strong, the blood
running warm in my veins. But as I ran I began to feel
that I wasn't alone. I couldn't shake the feeling...who
was there with me? I remember flashes of light and the
thin, jagged, white lines cracking the sky. The creek
began to toss and sing in a way that I had never heard
and I kept asking myself---who was there? Then it
came to me; it was nature herself, bare and open; she
was all around me, gusting in the wind, calling---I
could feel her riding my shoulder. The rain kept
coming, like tiny balls of crystal, each shattering into a
thousand pieces before soaking into the ground."

He paused for a moment. She saw the softness in
his eyes and could only wonder of this gentle, golden
man who lay before her.

"It was wonderful, Abby," he said, "and I hoped it
would never end. I ran on, feeling the rain across my
face. It felt pure and cool and everywhere I looked the

And The Mountains Cried

forest became a spread of green and from it, as if a voice, fresh and alive, I could hear it say, 'Keep running, Matt, keep running.' And I did...I kept running, not wanting to stop, not if it kept the earth like this. Then the thunder quit the sky, the rain faded and suddenly it was over. For me it seemed like the ending of a great song. I made a final run along the creek and turned for my cabin."

Abby saw his eyes looking into the night, as if lost in a faraway roll of thunder, his mind teetering on the meaning and balance of the words he had spoken.

He turned to her and said, "That's my home, Abby...that's where I live." Then he looked away and said no more, the expression on his face unmoving, distant, unaware of his silence. For a moment she felt as if erased out of being, non-existent. When she asked him if anything was wrong, he turned to her, surprised, and laughed softly.

"I've never felt better."

The words wrapped around her like the intimacy of a warm blanket and she felt everything was right, that she belonged just there, where she was, together with him. Their eyes met in a moment of understanding and they smiled, as if they were no longer separate people, their thoughts the same.

After a moment, she leaped to her feet and clasped her hands happily. "I'll be back in one minute, Matt." And, in a breathless rush, she got them two fresh glasses of iced tea. They breathed in the cool, fresh night air, laughed at nothing and at each other, cut off from the world, enclosed by darkness, and the pale yellow glow of the sky.

Once they heard a night hawk call out into the silence; a single, lonely cry that arched upward from a distant mountain, echoed along its massive rock ledges, across the sky...searching. A flash of lightning fell across the horizon, but there came no answer. The night fell silent

Abby looked out into the sky. It lay like a shimmering lake above the mountains. "It's so beautiful, Matt...I wish it would be like this always."

They stayed late into the night, talking, caressing, her skin against his, whispering, a gathering of broken sentences made whole by their wanting each other too much, of suffering and pain swept into intervals of desire and pleasure that come only once in a lifetime. They did not know when, but sometime before sunrise they fell asleep in each other's arms.

They went to dinner at a cafe, a small, quiet restaurant, hidden in the trees, with intimate booths. She wore a pale green dress, luxurious and fragile. It fell over one shoulder, and left the other bare.

The night passed in one of those enchanting hazes in which they wanted to remember every word, every glance, yet afterward nothing remained except the glow of the evening. They drank champagne, hands entwined across the table, two parts of one soul.

And The Mountains Cried

It was around midnight when they arrived at Abby's house. Matt waited quietly while she unlocked the door. They entered in silence, she turned on no lights. She walked him through the living room in shadowed darkness, unable to see the expression of his face, perceiving only the unbroken sound of their steps and her own feeling---that she wished to walk on and on, a feeling she could not define, but the odd glow she felt within told her that his face reflected the same feeling as hers.

She let her fingers drag along the textured cloth of the couch as they walked passed, a mindful awareness of the whole spread of their time together and that this was the room where they had first sat and talked.

As they climbed the wide staircase, she began to feel the blood surging through her veins, in her throat, and there came upon her a desire so strong that it seemed like agony. When they reached the landing she took his hand and led him through the open door of her bedroom. She let his hand drop and stepped away. He stood in the middle of the room, they were alone, with the wide glass doors open to the summer night and the unfolding light of a September moon.

She watched him draw nearer and, raising her head, felt his hands on her cheeks, lightly, holding her face in his fingertips. Then his fingers closed in her hair, drawing her to him, her legs pulled forward, her mouth open against his. He heard the moan of her breath and knew it was a moan of pleasure, a sound of surrender under the touch of his lips. He pulled away and she felt his hands easing her dress free from the curve of her shoulder. She was looking up at him, an all too human glance, meant to tell him that she was ready to submit to anything he wished her to do.

Without a word, he reached behind her and undid the back of her dress, its smooth folds sliding from her body and falling to the floor. Then he unhooked her bra. It was white and plain and woven with simple lace around the edges. She saw an instantaneous movement in the muscles of his face as the bra fell away, giving it a strange serenity, his lips drawn slightly, his eyes faintly glazed, his glance intent with the desire she knew resembled her own. He did not smile, but let his eyes gaze into hers, her skin glimmering in the fringed light.

The touch of his hands on her breast caused her to gasp; she felt his fingers pressing gently against her ribs and saw him lower his head down and brush the curve of her swollen nipples with his tongue.

She let her head fall back and closed her eyes, wanting to hold to the moment, as nothing else mattered, conscious of only the mindless hunger of her body, her soul, a hunger expressed without shame or consequence or right or wrong, forever. And whatever came to pass, whatever brutal reckoning was forced upon her in the future, there would always be this to remember.

And The Mountains Cried

She could hear her words from within: 'Yes, Matt, yes…now…like this…please, I want you, do it now…' She felt her body quiver and knew it was as it had to be, and was, and would always be---as proof, as sanction, as reward for all the past times that had been so hard to bear. She was thinking of it now and realized suddenly that he would be the only person with whom she had ever made love in this house, the place she had always thought to be her home.

Matt led her to the bed and they stood before each other. He watched as she stepped from her shoes, fetching from him some deeper force that moved not just his body, but his soul, that intolerable thought of their not being together always. She began to unbuttoned his shirt; then her hands moved from his shirt to his waist. She unbuckled his belt, then the top of his pants and rolled his shirt clear of his shoulders.

Outside the earth was streaked in moonlight. It seemed to remove all sound, as if within the expanding world there existed no other person. She laid herself down on the bed, the long line of her body extending across a green bedspread. She lay still, resting on the crook of her elbow and watched as he removed the rest of his clothes.

He kicked his clothes aside and stood by the edge of the bed, arms at his side, naked, looking down at her. He saw her shoulders move and stepped closer to the bed as she lifted herself up, her hand pressing into the bedspread and, with the hand yet free, extended her arm and closed her fingers around his erect flesh. She leaned her head forward and began to trace its length with the brush of her tongue, covering its rim with the warm wetness of her mouth, lips moving over the tight skin in slow, exquisite moans. She could feel his blood surging and his legs began to quiver. After a moment she let him go and lay back on the bed, her eyes half-closed in helpless anticipation.

He waited for only a moment, then laid down beside her. She lifted her hips and, with one easy move of his arm, he slid her panties gently down her legs. His eyes traveled down her body to the black triangle of hair between her legs. The sight of it moved him even further and he ran his hand over her body, feeling the eagerness of her movements. She threw her head back against the curve of his arm, breathless, clasping his hand and from somewhere within her there came a sound, a helpless, gasping moan; then her legs pulled forward and her hips began to rise upward in short, jerking shudders. She could feel his mouth on her breasts, the touch of his hard fingers pressing into her wetness.

"Please," she murmured, her eyes closed, lips apart, the sound of her voice struggling for the words, "I want you inside me."

For Abby it seemed the moment for which the earth was made. He moved on her with a curious power which she had never before known, kissing her, whispering soft words into her ear. She felt his hot surge enter her and pressed her face against him, her mouth moving along the curve of his neck, down his chest, his shoulder. She searched blindly for his mouth, knowing that every gesture of her desire was a tribute to all the steps of the years past, the steps down a course that had led her to this moment, a moment of such power and force that no other measure of her being seemed necessary.

His arms were around her now, pulling her into him, holding her, his flesh melting into her flesh, her bones. She felt his mouth on hers, her moaning cries breaking against the still air of the room. It was as if he had taken possession of her every fiber. She felt him shaking and arched herself into him.

Then she felt it, an explosive shudder rushing to her center, surging, spreading in waves to the furthest reaches of her body. She screamed in pleasure, in agony, holding him to her until all within her seemed drained and they meshed inextricably into one.

She lay still, feeling the weight of his body on hers, unable to move, her mouth open. She heard the gasps of his breathing and knew it was the sound of his spent desires, his pleasure; that she had given that to him. She cried out, softly, breathlessly, "Oh, Matt, why didn't you find me sooner."

C H A P T E R 1 7

The next morning they awoke late. Matt felt he should be happy, and so, in a way, he was. Abby was beside him, the soft warmth of her body cradled next to his, her fragrance---the fragrance of a mountain spring itself filling the air; they were together. Yet something troubled him, and no matter how he tried to turn his mind away from it, to dismiss the thought, it remained with him.

After dressing she watched him as he made his way about the room. She could feel something in his manner and thought of what he had given to her, of their time together. She could still feel her blood moving, as if energy flowing through a maze of intricately laid wires, an alternating rhythm that bound her heart to his.

He stood at the far end of the bedroom, next to the windows, looking not at her, but out into a bright blue sky, when he heard her call his name, her voice quiet and gentle.

He turned and saw the reflection of her next words on her face and could guess the rest. He knew then the reason for his uneasiness. It seemed out of time, but he knew they had reached the edge, the edge of that hollow space whose other side they had yet to see.

The look on his face was one Abby did not recognize, as if something precious, beyond that which he had ever known, was about to be lost. He looked away, pausing, not wanting to break the peacefulness of the morning---of what he knew was coming.

"Can't this wait, Abby?"

She gazed at him, held momentarily silent by the anxious note in his voice and knew he was feeling her thoughts.

"Oh, Matt..." Her voice echoed helplessly against the walls, trying to push away what had to be; push it away for another time, another place, but it kept moving between them and they knew it had to happen.

"What are we going to do?" he asked, his head jerking in defense of a reply.

Her eyes closed, feeling something tearing at her insides. She walked to the side of the bed, keeping her eyes to the floor, allowing the slowness of her steps to delay time a few seconds longer; to gain the strength needed for this moment, a moment that was to be the rule of all their coming days.

Her eyes moved to his as a question, but saw only pain and knew he had no answer. She took a moment to look at him as he stood before her, as if to hold the full sight of his figure, wanting, in that instant, to do nothing more, fighting against the pressure of her thoughts, because she knew she was not ready---would never be ready. He was the only man she'd ever loved, the only man she ever wanted to love. Then, as if broken by the whole of what was to come, and of their time together, and with tears in her eyes, she turned away. "I don't know," she said. Her voice was faint as a breath of air.

Matt stood before her, feeling an emotion held by their years apart: a loneliness beyond the moment, beyond the silence of the room, as if his mind was suddenly reduced to a single thought and he was sensing something forming before him that was unstoppable. "I know you're afraid," he said, "but if we let this go, if we pretend we never met, then I don't think we'll ever get another chance." He reached out, his hand brushing her cheek. "We still have the rest of our lives."

When she looked up at him, her face held a reflection of despair; she seemed to be struggling with some force outside of herself. It seemed to her, and had always seemed, that some things were simply destined to happen and could never have been otherwise. She felt herself tremble from the thought and would tremble later from the pain, but, at this moment, knew that never would she feel regret for her love of Matt Callahan.

She shook her head. "John is hardly lucid…" she said, her voice jerking unevenly. "…he could never understand, his mind has gone beyond that." She shut her eyes tight and buried her face in her hands, shaking her head. "Oh, God, why didn't we meet earlier?"

After a moment she raised her head and said, "I always dreamed of meeting someone like you. But once I was married the thought frightened me, because I was afraid this would happen. I don't know how I knew, only that it is the one thing given me not to understand until now. John is a good man and I care about what happens to him, but he could never make me feel as you have. You're like something I've never known."

He made a movement to speak, but she motioned him down. "Wait, let me finish. It's like your right inside of me and I can hear your voice and feel your breath. Without you I'll be alone and lost. You're my dream come true, my magic, my passion for living. These are things I've never felt for John. I know now I shouldn't have married him for the reasons I did; it wasn't enough. There was always something missing, but now he's older, and sick, and it would kill him if I were to leave."

Matt Callahan stood silent, the sun refracting off the glass doors behind him in weaving circles of light, as if the moment was marked by a faceless clock that held no time and the beginning and the end had run together. He had listened to the words, but could not connect them into sentences. Nothing made sense. He felt very cold and then there came the sound of his voice. It rolled from his throat as unfamiliar and desperate as ever she had heard.

"Abby, I can't let you go. I'll remain with you in however way you like…as your husband or your lover, secretly or openly. I'll take a room in some town near Monterrey, just so I can see you…it won't matter when or where."

She reached out to him, wanting to speak and he saw the faint movement of her mouth. It was not a smile, but a silent cry from within.

"I love you, Abby," he said quietly, and she could see the suffering in his face, "…as I love my life, you're the shape of my world, my existence, my reason to live, my being, my soul. I've loved you from the moment I saw you walking through the crowded restaurant. I loved you when we stood by the ruins of Juan's childhood home. I loved you on the terrace of your home, and I've loved you on all the days that followed."

She closed her eyes. "Oh, Matt, I…" Her voice was a half gasp, half moan.

"Let me finish, darling. If we're what we have been to each other, then come back to Texas with me. We can start again from where we are now. Do it for our sake or for whatever reason, but come with me. It's our time, give us this one chance to be together. Don't throw us away."

Matt saw her leaning back against the bed, saw the slender figure that seemed to sway, like the broken stem of a flower, then gather all its strength to remain standing. She was looking straight at him, the plea of his words dissolved within her eyes, filling them with tears.

"Matt, if you ask me to get a divorce, to forget my past life, to feel no concern, no responsibility, no guilt, just to exist for us, for you, for our need for each other, I'd do it. You're the love I've always wanted long before I knew you existed. You're the fuel of my body, my necessity and I love you more than the air I breath. This is the only way you deserve to be loved and the only way I want you to love me. Once you told me that you heard my footsteps as I came up behind you and that it made you smile and, as I got closer, your smile grew and that you could not quit smiling. I never want you to feel differently about me. If I were to leave now and become your wife, those thoughts would haunt me. I'd be afraid of turning into someone other than the woman you have come to love, that your feelings for me would fade and soon you'd not love me at all. And that you'd come not to like yourself for making me leave someone that has no strength, no capacity to fight back. It would only destroy the spirit I love so much in you. That's why I don't want you to stop me…let me go back. I don't know how I'll live through the days to come, but I will."

She walked to him and gently touched his arm, as if to take away the hurt she saw in his face and whispered, "I'd go with you, Matt, because of my own selfish feelings, because of my love and need for you, but please don't make me do that."

She heard a sound that rose from the depth of his core, like something ripped from his gut. He tried to speak, but couldn't, and began to cry. She took his hands in hers; saw the hurt confessed in the slump of his tall, ascetic figure, a helpless surrender to a stabbing swirl of emotion that he could not control. Tears welled in her eyes; she felt his pain, felt her own.

"Matt, my dearest Matt," she whispered, kissing his hands.

He stood hunched against the glass doors, his head dropping downward in short little jerks, until his eyes were looking at the floor. Then something drew up in his throat, faintly at first, like a small discoloration, it fell down through his middle, carving his insides, spinning, peeling away all control. He felt himself tremble, feeling sick and struggled within himself to understand what she had said, as if the words she spoke were words not his to comprehend.

He took a long breath before he could look at her again and said, "Abby, I don't know if I can do this. I can live with any reality except a world without you.

And The Mountains Cried

To give you up, to never see you again, seems beyond acceptance."

The words seemed to split him open. He looked at her, waiting, trying to hold on, fearing the moment for what it brought. Then he reached for her and they held each other, feeling the pain of what could never be.

That night they went to Abby's house for dinner, each knowing what the other was thinking, knowing only that it was a thought neither wanted to mention. She was making a new rice and chicken dish. The rice had been cooking for only a short time. She was dicing a pepper when he came up behind her, put his arms around her and kissed her lightly on her neck and whispered again that he loved her. She felt something move inside, something deep and just for a moment, as impossible as it seemed, she felt that everything was going to be okay.

"You're working too hard," he said.

Abby knew that the meaningless chit-chatter was simply a way to avoid talking about the obvious, trying to help her in whatever way he could. It made her feel even closer to him.

There were delicious smells about, baked chicken, guacamole, tomatoes, taco shells frying crisp in the twilight air. They turned off the ceiling lights, lit two candles and ate at the little breakfast table next to the kitchen. The dinner was perfect and after they finished, had a glass of wine. She was wearing a dress cut just above her knees, beige with short sleeves. She laughed softly, her dark eyes sparkling in the low light of the candle and Matt thought how beautiful she was and gave her a smile that was both loving and sad, knowing this was the beginning of their end.

That night they lay in bed together, touching, whispering, making love until almost sunrise. It was as it had to be, a joining of two pleading bodies, an act of surrender made more complete by their denial of the words they had spoken that morning. They had little time for sleep, each giving to the other, suspending the few fleeting hours they had together. It was an act of passion, of suffering; it was a moment made of desire, a moment that broke over the room in cries of agony and pleasure, through the open glass doors, across the terrace, rode the wind into the vast, silent blackness of night and the dreadful reckoning that was yet to come. Sometime just before dawn, they fell into an exhausted sleep.

The early high clouds had already burned away when Abby awoke. As she opened her eyes she felt a slight jolt of surprise finding herself alone. She lay on the bed looking through the heavy glass doors, blinking against the brightness; sunrays burning through the clear air, striking the terrace floor. The floor seemed not a color, but a spread of light shimmering in the sun, a light produced from shifting waves of heat rising out of the clay tiles, like invisible flames.

And The Mountains Cried

She moved her tongue along the roof of her mouth, hearing a muffled moan in her throat. It was not the sound, but the sudden flash of reality that opened her eyes wide. She raised herself up, leaning awkwardly on her forearm, the weight of the sheet light on her naked body. There was a delicate silence in the room. Then she heard faint sounds coming from downstairs and knew it must be Matt. She wondered how he had gotten up without waking her, but it didn't matter. She thought only that she must see him. She slipped out of bed, dressed quickly, and went downstairs.

She found Matt waiting, sitting motionless in the light of a lamp. It was as she remembered him the first day he came to her house---a white linen shirt, beige pants.

He had not heard her when she first approached, then he glanced up at her and smiled, but the effort wasn't convincing.

She stood looking at him, some steps away. Neither of them spoke, as if strangers in an empty room. He swallowed and she saw a slight jerking motion in his throat.

"I thought I'd let you sleep," he said.

Abby nodded faintly.

There was silence. Their time together had been brief. It was all they had lived for, nothing beyond.

"I made some coffee."

She shook her head, wanting to go to him, but was afraid to move, feeling drained, weightless, fearing she would be swept away by even the slightest movement. Matt saw her distress. She closed her eyes listening to the sound of his steps moving toward her, as if the sounds held all that was possible, granting her the dreams for which there was no place, no time, no permanence of being other than now.

He stood before her, unable to speak, knowing that neither of them could conceal the meaning of their silence, as if caught in a chill seeking warmth. She heard the slow ending softness of his breath and slowly looked up at him, her lips half open and, like a lost soul, reached out and fell into the circle of his arms, burying her head in his chest.

The air in the room seemed heavy, as if it had no life and she began to cry. He felt her shaking and held her tightly to him, nudging her face with his, pressing gently with his lips, brushing away the tears. Then he moved his face along the wetness of her cheeks and placed his mouth over hers. She clung to him, feeling the natural flex and strain of his body, as if all the joy and reason and meaning of life were offered to her in this room, at this moment and nothing could begrudge her otherwise. He cradled her face in his hands and kissed her gently.

After a moment, he pulled away and smiled at her, a faint half-smile, gave a little shrug and said, "I guess I better be going." There was a slight tremor in the sound of his voice, but he kept smiling.

Their time together had sped past them, soundlessly; a shadowed hollowness now wedging between them, pushing the light from their hearts. Her mind began to race; broken bits of thought flew past her. Everything was moving too fast. 'Don't leave, Matt, not now, not ever.' She could hear her voice crying out from somewhere within. He took her hand and led her through the front door.

Outside the day was cloudless, flowers hung still in the air, transformed by the heat. They walked together, her arm pressed to his, the strike of their shoes echoing against the high stone wall surrounding the garden. The path ran unevenly, rising slightly in a narrow curve around the heavy stone bench.

"Matt, would you mind…could we stop for a little while longer, pretend everything is okay, just to talk and be together a few moments more for all the years we missed…"

The walls enclosed the garden, cutting them off from the street, from the world beyond. At the top of the path, in a cluster of red roses, they sat down on the stone bench. She pressed herself close to him, looking out across the garden, the clear pools of water throwing the slanting sun back to the sky in sharp gleams of light.

In the midst of the brightness, Matt turned to her. Her eyes rose to his and she saw the pain he felt, yet within his eyes was a dim reflection of the look she had seen on the day of their first meeting, as if he were trying to regain possession of the time they had spent together, of this moment, and everything that had led them to it: of life's past, its present, and how life hadn't been too much, really, a few years, but this woman at his side---this woman whom he loved--- would be forever with him.

"Are you sorry we met, Abby?"

The shudder she felt was like a cry of helplessness; she lay back against him, with closed eyes. "I'm only sorry for the life we missed." Then she lifted her hands and put her arms around his neck. "Oh, Matt, I had to find you...hold me close, we're together now."

A lone car drove by, its sound muffled by the garden wall, hardly distinguishable. They were alone, drowning in their senses, drawn down in an undercurrent of loss and grief...and despair. "Matt," she whispered; "Matt." She repeated his name again and again, a thin, lost sound, as if she were afraid something had already stolen him away.

He did not speak, but pulled her closer, feeling only the presence of her in his arms. She squeezed him tighter and heard the choking stress of his voice as he began to speak.

"I'll always be here, Abby...don't be afraid. Maybe I won't see you in the future, but know that you're in my thoughts and I'll be beside you in spirit always."

And The Mountains Cried

She did not know if a minute had passed or an hour. Everything seemed part of everything else, the heat and Matt and the sobs that racked her body. She told him she'd been wrong, that she would go back to Texas with him and that she couldn't live without him.

He listened in silence, his hand gently stroking her hair. When she could cry no more, he lifted her face to his, and when he kissed her it seemed the summation of all their time together, and an end that neither could accept. Then he placed her hand in his and rose from the bench. She wanted to follow, but he shook his head and backed away, their fingers losing their hold little by little until they no longer touched. Then he turned and walked to the gate. Abby wiped her eyes, tears and sunlight blurring her vision.

When he got to the end of the path he put his hand on the latch, pushed the gate open and took a step back. He could see her still sitting on the bench, eyes wet with tears, helpless, and in that one quiet, still moment neither of them moved, they just looked at each other across the gulf of air---a gulf over which they would never pass again.

Then he turned and walked to his van. She heard the gate close behind him; the sound cut her breath and she felt her body quiver, as if some small amount of time had to pass before she could believe it. She sat curled down within herself, her face in her hands and there came from somewhere a voice that whispered, "Oh, God, no."

Greg Gannaway

A dove dipped low over the garden, gray, like a fluttering piece of ash against the thick stone wall. She heard the start of the engine; heard it idle quietly for a moment...and then the wheels of his van rolled away into the distance and he was gone.

And The Mountains Cried

Matt didn't sleep that night and went to the site early the next morning to meet with Juan. It would be their last day together.

By late afternoon the shadows were long and slanting. They sat together along the bank of the little creek, its sounds merging into the finely grained mist above. The mist seemed always there and always disappearing, like small voices flickering in the air. Juan glanced at Matt. He was sitting bent forward, motionless, leaning on his forearms, his two hands clasped together, looking into the shimmering wetness, listening, hearing the voices, hearing their message, unaware of Juan and the earth around him, as if the whole world had turned to water. It was the time when everything that was to happen had happened and nothing remained to be said.

Matt did not see the concern that closed over Juan's face, nor did he hear the words when he asked, "Are you okay, Champ?"

The slanting shadows lengthened, reaching over the creek, rising along the slope of the land until they crossed the road.

"It's getting late, Ol Buddy…I better get packed."

"Sure, Champ."

Then, as they rose to leave, Matt said, "I wish I could make it back someday after it's built."

At the time Juan was surprised by the statement, but later realized that the little creek somewhere, somehow must have told him that there would be no such trip.

They met early the next morning at the site. The sky was gray, heavy, pressing down on the mountains, a light drizzle had begun to fall, sifting through the raw levels of mountain air. They spoke with a faint tinge of sadness, moving off and past one thing to another, rehashing the rich and warm memories they'd shared.

Suddenly there was thunder, it filled the slopes like a great locomotive, rolling and rumbling behind the mountains, a storm driving from the south, out of Mexico City, along the gulf waters, dark with the beginning of fall.

They spoke for only a short time longer, then Matt shook the rain from his shoulders and walked to his van. As he drove away he watched his friend recede in the rearview mirror, hat in hand, waving. The road

And The Mountains Cried

curved south toward the gathering clouds breaking over the mountains. He slowed his van at the crest of a small hill and looked back beyond the trees. In the distance he could still see the hazy outline of his old friend, a soft grayish color, like fog, standing in the hollow of the road. He looked for a long moment, until slowly the rain washed away the wholeness of his figure and everything floated up and away into the sky. Matt tapped down on the accelerator and headed for Texas. He would never see Juan or Mexico again.

Construction of the houses began in early fall and ran through the beginning of summer the following year. During the winter months, the weather would change abruptly. Those without a home huddled together for warmth, sleeping where they could, on a park bench, along a wooded path, in pitiful clothing, without food or love, without care or shelter, each seeking to keep their heart beating for just another day.

From time to time they would hear from a passing stranger the brief mention of the houses; it would stir their hearts and they would look at each other with sudden feelings of hope. They were the very old who, in their blurred and dissolving world, could not remember a day of happiness and believed that those whom God cared for most didn't go about wanting things; or the young, who had never had anything--- never really anything they wanted, as for a house...

They did not know about construction, they knew nothing of design, they knew only that Juan had fought against great odds and was now succeeding. They had once believed in the whispered voices that said the houses would never be built---and yet, when they heard that the project was moving forward, they savored the moment, feeling their future, and that of those to follow, would be made better.

Matt had designed the project as a composition in rectangles. Each house, of concrete, stucco and glass, was a model of simple structural components; there were no superfluous moldings, no ornaments, none was needed, the beauty came from the simplicity of the structure.

In July the project was completed. Juan had built it in only nine months. On the morning after its completion, he arrived at the site early as he always did, a still, brilliant sunlight falling full on his face; it held the combined look of achievement and reward.

He took only a few steps before stopping, standing alone on the empty road, looking across the site, his eyes bright and alive, as if seeing some impossible vision from another world. What he saw were houses, the houses he had built; they stood scattered amongst the trees, on the ridges, along the banks of the little creek. He smiled, it was the houses that had been the immovable thought in his mind and, as time went by,

it was always the houses at the center of his focus. He
continued to smile, knowing he wanted to look at
them, to keep looking, to always look, because the
sense of life he was now feeling would be forever
bound to them, a moment uniting his beginning to the
completion of his goal.

He closed his eyes and went on, suspending the
moment for a few minutes longer. Then it hit him: a
rush of emotion that he could not contain and, in the
spark of that moment, his hands shot into the air
above his head, arms waving against the sky, as if he
was receiving an ovation, an ovation not only for
himself, but for every man that had helped him
complete his dream.

"Thank you," he shouted, "thank you."

The houses stood like motionless gifts lifted from
the earth, spreading in soft broken lines with the rise
and fall of the land. When entering the houses, one
could feel the space enclose about them, each structure
a place of joy and quiet excitement. Trees rose over
them like umbrellas of protection; but now they had
something else to protect, the people who had moved
into the houses, who moved about on the sidewalks,
down the grassy slopes, relaxed in the swimming
pools, ran to the tops of rising walls and sat under the
wide shade of the trees, dangling their feet in the little
creek that seemed to come from nowhere. There was a
new sense of hope and promise, like flowers unfolding

from the first touch of sunlight. It was as Juan had always dreamed.

A week had passed since the project's completion. The idle time gave Juan plenty of time for reflection. He liked to sit on one of the benches by the little creek and watch the glow of the day rise in the east, spread across the sky, and fade and die behind the mountains. He watched all the life around him, the joggers, the bicyclers, and the people walking along the trails. People forgot, for a little while, life's endless troubles and began to enjoy the gentle evenings, the dream of peace, their homes, and being with those they loved.

That summer was beautiful, an assault on ones senses, wild flowers shooting up through the grass, cluttering around the bench where Juan liked to sit. He would feel his heart grow warm and sometimes pick a few just to remember the day. Then he would turn away uncomfortably and swear, as if trying to put his masculinity back together.

When Matt telephoned him from Texas and said, "No…no particular reason, just wondered how you were getting along…haven't heard from you in a week or so," the sound of Juan's voice made him feel that something wasn't quite right.

At around noon, three days later, Matt was sitting at his kitchen table having lunch. He was buttering his second biscuit, when the telephone rang. He got up, walked to his desk and lifted the receiver. After only a moment he let it drop, unable to escape the cold, radiant clarity of what he had been told.

In the early morning hours of that same morning, Juan Sanchez awoke in the stillness of a sun filled room. It fell through the windows, across the wood floor, striking squarely the stucco walls with its brightness. The man who had once moved with ease through rough, torn construction sites, now lay quietly on his pillow, his arms resting obediently at his sides, feeling too weak to get out of bed. Through the wide windows of his room was the blue sky, his green garden, the live oaks. How he had enjoyed being outdoors in the warm sun when he was young and all of life stretched before him. Now his mind was hazy, drifting, his tired body swept up in a maze of memories. Slowly he saw through his window, not the quiet, blue sky or his garden, but those lasting images of distant times.

Light flashed across his eyes, fluttered. "Is that you, Matt?" he said aloud. Matt's face drifted above him, drifted away.

That Matt was not with him now saddened him so that he began to feel a desolate emptiness of a kind he had never known before. He cleared his throat and told himself to go to sleep; morning thoughts are best. Then he closed his eyes and lay breathing peacefully, as if seeing the bright little flowers of his garden, delicate and delicious in the sun. After a moment he appeared to have thought of something else; and, raising his head slightly, he drew in a breath of air and gazed out through his window into the darkness. "Yes," he murmured, "in the morning the sun will shine and I will feel differently about everything." Then he lowered his head and went to sleep.

The next morning was beautiful and peaceful. The windows of Juan's bedroom stood open to his green garden, and the sun hung bright and quiet in the sky. He opened his eyes only once, a slight smile on his lips, then closed them forever. He had lived to see his dream built. He died in the gentle dawn, with the sun shining on his face, two weeks after its completion.

And The Mountains Cried

C H A P T E R   1 9

Summer came early to Chipinque the following year, the dazzling colors of spring fading in the heat. It was late afternoon; the sky seemed of another blue, a summer blue, and the sun, too, was growing brighter, breaking through billowing clouds in thin slices of yellow. A light wind had begun to blow from the south, across the trees; it brought the smell of green earth. People took leisurely walks in the park, arm in arm, taking time to talk to those they passed and to each other. There was a gentleness in the air.

Abby stood on the terrace of her mountain home, listening, hearing only the sway of leaves in the soft breeze. The city lay far below, an explosion of tiny, half-dissolved shapes, marching into the sky. It had been a year since her last visit.

She thought---letting her eyes rest on the little houses far below---that if she had nothing of him, nothing but the memories, here he still was, offered to her, to be seen and touched, like the final expression of some great force; his, as his spirit, as his soul; here were the houses he had created, hers for this moment, hers by the splendor of their existence.

Suddenly her eyes stopped along a grassy ridge. It was the place where she and Matt had once sat. The sight was like the touch of his hand and of many things beyond. She took from it their last day together. She could almost feel his cheek pressed against hers, his words hanging in the air, as if she were hearing them again: "Abby," he had said, "it's okay, whatever happens, we will always be together…somewhere."

Tears welled in her eyes and for some minutes she could only stand without moving, her mind falling back to a memory more real than what was before her. "Matt," she whispered quietly, "there is only one love…nothing will change that."

Then, slowly, the moment slipped away and her eyes began to move across the site, never quite stopping, gliding from one house to another, along the ridges, to another, and another. They were as he had told her, but she could not grasp a sense of scale and it seemed as if she could reach over the stone railing and pick any one of them up with her fingers. Her hand moved absently, following their form along the rolling landscape, feeling a physical sense of closeness, feeling it for him, for herself. Light streamed from their windows, through the trees and into the sky. It was a comforting sight, alive with the pulse of life.

She closed her eyes, a faint shudder at the end of her vision, as if the houses and she and Matt were now as one, joined together in a way for which there seemed no words, indefinably. She could feel the memories flooding through her. She let them come, she always let them come, the days all mingling and swimming together in a single silence. She thought of the man that had made it possible, felt the weight of his memory, so indelibly etched in her heart forever. Why they had met or how it had come about she did not know. She knew only that it was meant to be, that the strands of her life were now woven with his and not time nor distance could part them completely; for wherever he was on this earth, there too was a part of her.

He had once said: "There are many ways to reach your dreams, Abby…just remember they hold all possibilities and are the magic of your life."

Together, they had found that magic…it was theirs forever.

Greg Gannaway

ABOUT THE AUTHOR

Greg Gannaway graduated from the school of architecture at the University of Houston. He was born in Austin, Texas and has lived there all of his life.

www.ingramcontent.com/pod-product-compliance
Lightning Source LLC
Chambersburg PA
CBHW070615130626
46556CB00001B/370